Exoneratio Dei

60809

0. Read Closely. Freedom is a religious word. It was a thought. In a brain somewhere. When a chemical did a thing in a place, somehow. A man woke and stood and began to move. He draped a cloth over his body. A cloth, made of a plant which was once alive in a place where it was killed. Like the piece of toast that he wanted to eat but couldn't heat in a toaster that was broken.

He left his home, a home like a thousand others, without eating a thing. And, though they were invisible, a thousand million lines spun about him. All because of the chemicals moving in the brain with the body of a man built around it. Those thousand million lines merged seamlessly with a thousand million more when little secret blue sparks and spinning metals purred his car to life. From a perspective, they were one as they moved along a road, which was like a thousand others, which were all connected. From one place to another. Both dots on the map of a larger place. A square upon a sphere called the globe.

Blood dripped from a broken artery in the neck of a man along the roadside. The red pool grew on the ground until it was too large. Until an arm stretched from the puddle and reached for the ditch. A ditch which fed a stream, then a pond and a river, for maybe a thousand miles, then a lake and a waterfall. Where a glial creature had placed a wheel.

The wheel spun when it caught the pool, which was no longer red, and electricity shot from its center. Like lightning, with no thunder, along a thousand wires, a thousand miles, into a thousand homes, like a thousand more.

In one of these homes, a man spoke into a machine. It changed his voice. Sent it coursing through the air. Past migrating fowl and bi-planes. While a faraway star heated the ground and set the winds to racing. Over a heaving molten ocean and a core of churning metal. Below orbiting satellites. Sent it coursing. Past weather-balloons and jet-streams. Until it reached the brain, in the man, in the car, on the road, like a thousand other roads, which were all connected. Until his wife got into the car and heard that their toaster was broken.

Amongst all the pathways, the neurons, the forces. Amongst all the order of a seeming chaos, which had not always been but which had grown into being. Amongst all the information travelling as spinning lines along roads and wires and migration routes, up to satellites, from faraway stars. A thought arose. Which is no more absurd than a creature, who might happen to be a human, having one of their own.

"Freedom is a religious word," was the thought, or so Sally imagined as she leaned out her window and stared at the people and the cars, between the buildings, and the sun and a sky crossed with jet-trails.

"So is this:

1. Water and meat between men. A virus-riddled mess of a man sits in a coffee shop hoping for some brilliant terrible event to take his mind off himself. His selves and all their conflicting nonsense. The look in his eyes will bring him no good. He doesn't doubt this or resist. Some men are able to surf the flow of their lives. Others have no choice but to go limp and tumble with the break.

He's writing a novel about himself. It's written in the third person. He intends to lie. He came to the café in order to write but nothing intelligible has come out of him so far. Just the same patterns of clicks and beeps that amount to everyone around him. He hears screams in the spaces between conversations and tries to keep from crying. His longtime friend owns the café he's sitting in. She doesn't know. He hasn't told anyone. Except the man who fucked it into him. Which was like telling no one at all. And a handful of strangers he's met along the way. Just to see.

He stands atop the only thing and must choose in which direction to jump. A man, skilled at finding the continuums between things, can't function with only one point to work from and a directionless will. He's scared, more scared than he's ever been, that this time he won't be able to make sense of it. He's been chasing down crows he's imagined. They've led him in circles. Like vultures would. Which makes him think that there's death nearby. And creatures who feast on it. Though he prays it's only the desert ascending.

Suddenly there are eyes there that weren't there before. In the form of some new sense of his, tingling. The weight of one more stare barely hunches him. He stands, as he's stood in the past, looks toward the sun and begins to walk, dragging his life along like a sentence he's grudgingly agreed to bear. He wonders what's been done to him. And by whom.

Opposing wills stop him at the first crossroads. He loses the sun. It's raining. Thoughts he needn't think and ones he needs to. Sewn into him like the seams of something torn apart. His ideas of love and life were learned from the man who fucked him dead. He'd innocently constructed them so long ago. Only recently to disassemble. Both defined by their opposite. As is everything there is. And isn't.

He's being forced to dissociate perspectives. To allow for the simultaneous existence of conflicting things. All he is, any longer, is the force keeping these things apart. Lest they annihilate. He's exhausted down to his cold cold bones. Always drinking in the sun's light as it spews out all that is, unable to generate his own, then pouring it into his virus-riddled lover, bartering in trade. Light for light. Exchanged in the flicker of men.

He needs help and he knows it. The only words in his blank black sketchbook are, "mommy, daddy, I'm not alright." But he's past the point where he can ask for it. Crossed that line. And he's kind of settled into a strange curiosity about where it all might lead.

When they shouted that one word, he woke up loudly. To find himself aleap in the air. Not quite ready to unfurl what he imagines must be wings. Hopefully. Black wings. So he has to have faith. Just enough to lean into the wind. Faith in a universe he doesn't trust anymore. For now. He doesn't need to know what he has to do. He knows that he just has to do it.

And he knows that he knows that he knows. Negation by multiplication. He digs the hole as deep as it'll go until he finds that he's no longer himself. And can possibly see himself clearly. Which is entirely impossible to a mind as rational as his. One so brazenly methodical that it has a tendency to hurl him from things just to be sure which way is down. Cause if that's down. Then that's up. The rest of it can spiral like a top for all he cares.

What other men drag as history, he maintains as aspects of expressions. So everyone can read his mind while he reads his plays aloud. His craft is maintaining that continuity. His art is explaining aspects of fascinating things. He's labyrinthine. Trying to find his way out.

Unless he treats his skin like a glove on some invisible hand sensing, he gets lost to it. He's smart enough to be as convincing as he is easily convinced. Every debate becomes a quick conversation between a genius and a fool. Any shift of the balance gets centrifugal and thunders through his life like a wrecking ball. He's chained to things. When he falls, it's a cartoon scramble to crush or be crushed, to watch him die or to die for him. Either way, two years ago, he shattered his heel when he jumped off a cliff because he was too afraid to fall from it. The wound will always tingle and never heal. Reminding him that he likes to fall. And which way is down.

This is where it begins.

Or you could go back six years, to the first man who touched him with force enough to unleash the geysers that introduced him to the sky. And made him long for earth. With force enough to carry years past his attention. Fraught with beatings and drooling invalids, destruction, infection and a bodiless will toward death, claiming bodies in some mindless tumbling, presumably hoping to stave off its own.

Six years or not, there's really only one moment. What it's been and what it becomes. The same way your reality is just a formulated thought. The same way a forty-year-old woman on ecstasy at a rave will tell you to cherish it. This moment woke to find a newly infected man trying to find words to explain, to no one he would ever know, why he's a good man and what his ruin says about the world.

It's not enough to be the best, the smartest, the most likely to succeed. Those people are the first to realize that they're living in dissonance. The difference between who and what we are. If ever we're the dreamed of ones, then never we the dreamers. He was left alone to reconcile the power he could imagine with the power he could wield. Resting in the eyes of his maker.

The loss of his innocence has stunted him since he noticed it. And the price he's paid is the passage of time, indifferently carrying on a purpose beyond him. Everything he's ever known, every two pieces put together, has told him that he's special. He can't explain why he hasn't been spared. This is the hardest truth for him to stand. Even with all his devices. It makes him fragile. What's worse, it makes him common.

A world underneath a world he'd known all his life, now with small creatures inside changing everything, forcing the realization that we're, all of us, rotting. And that life's what's keeping the meat from stinking. Life's just one of the things that water does. First flows the water then beats the heart. Water's just a tendency of hydrogen. Hydrogen's the balance of positive and not positive. And there it is. So a tired man sets his mind.

He vows to make the worst choices, the choices no one else would ever make, just to do something, anything, to further it onward. It's his lazy, heroic attempt at martyrdom. And the only real way he's connected to anyone at all. By the myths he tells himself from what sense he can make of the world.

Terrified of the brand new intensity to everything, instead of admitting that he's become paper-thin, he adds more nonsense to his history. Concocts a heretic religion based on all that he can figure, believing that when a man reaches a point where he begins to consider wishing away his past, he creates a loop in space and time. It takes him back to the moment when he first chose but leaves him unable to change a thing. Just witness and relive, over and over, what he's already endured. His future becomes a collection of probabilities. And he's lost to his horrors redoubling indefinitely.

All he really wants to do is get stoned. Just enough to hear his own voice over all the screaming. So he can begin to knit his life back together. Which is just a bunch of pretty words. He has a gift when it comes to telling stories. That's really all his life is anymore. Poetics intended to take what is inexcusably vulgar and to word it just right.

Enough to make his parents proud. Which is the effort of taking the word *truth* through *belief* into *perception* past *conception* into *story,* which is a lie.

Understand, he's a condemned man. A prison he's excavated from the ruins of all he's ever known. A Babylonian prison for demons. His heart and his mind are both made of meat. And his lover's a fire elemental who got its foot caught inside a man. He senselessly loves a man whose role in the circle of life is to calculate pi to the last digit, like a rolling autistic. Or its equivalent. One man on a quest for the perfect irrational and one man trying to explain it. If only to forgive him.

If these pages aren't evidence enough of something broken, this is what's on his mind as he swaggers with a lungful of reefer, holding it in until all the oxygen's gone and he can conceive of the opening of another eye: The four a.m. call he ignored, begging for a ride. He wonders if he's finally strong enough to let there be some obvious reflection of how alone they really are. How alone they are together with his disease.

"I take back my heart." He says it out loud. To no one who matters. To anyone who can hear. But it isn't *his* heart, any longer, insofar as he'd given it away. When he took it back and ran away with it, it was only someone else's something he stole, any longer.

2. Equal and opposite to something catastrophic. Only in the deepest night did he dare take it back. Then, with a newly stolen heart, J wandered. He had to get away, with his reclaimed loot, lest the heart in his pocket keep craving. Away from M. The man at first consumed by, then devoted to, his own grotesqueries. It's what first drew them together. J couldn't resist the rhapsody of M's torments. Agonies intent on dragging whosoever along. Whosoever might be fool enough, with hearts enough to crave and minds enough to hasten something doomed. It couldn't be more obvious.

J's the sad genius who spins and spins. Each time coming close enough to full circle to be convinced that it all just spirals. He's okay with this. Fool enough to think that anything spiraling must lead to somewhere sublime. When, instead, the wound, as it all unwound, was a mortal one, bleeding light. Unraveling the pattern of him. Separating the meat from the man and leaving parts out. This is his version of completeness, as near as he can construct it, even though he's evaporating.

There comes a time, and the time always comes, when he'll finally understand his ability to genesis and, for a time, he'll think he's free. After an indefinite time of being caged. Followed by a time of heroic blame, wondering what sort of god would put a man in a cage with an animal that vicious. Suddenly seeing himself on a continuum, he'll feel powerful and small.

For now, no matter the tumble, the scramble, the plummet from the sky, J always leans toward M. Always from the chest, subliming. Constantly disassembling structures he'd never had time to build. Being archeologically human. Unearthing artifacts of paradigm and character while consentlessly being readily scavenged. His lover is a scavenger virus, encoded to carelessly and ceaselessly take. Blackhole-like. Just as love is much like gravity.

They are a sun and a blackhole on opposite sides of a wormhole, both afraid to bear the distortions of space and time it would take to be together. Cosmically reaching only to tear each other apart. Beyond biological, beyond chemical, their bond is a physical one. An essential quantum force exerted. Like ink to words on a page.

J, the silly clever fool, believes that this is his only. If only he can figure out a way. All he ever does is try to figure a way out. Wrapped up in a sentence he can't properly word. Knowing that a man preoccupied is safe harbor to no other and is easily reclaimed by the sea without something solid to hold onto. Unless he can learn to navigate what, for him, is oceanic. This is the crux of it. His terrible genius growing bored while his compulsions threaten to exceed his capabilities.

His, to bestow, is clarity. He has the ability to say things perfectly. Though he hates the things he can easily explain. As much as he hates and loves what he cannot fathom. Or whom. Which mostly leaves him, at the extents of himself, staring off into obscurities.

Those things behind him blur with those things before. He spends his time trying to create godforms from all the spare truths he's managed to scavenge. So sure of his wicked blasphemy that he closes his eyes at the end of each invocation he mutters to bring these monstrous things to life.

He holds his breath. Then flips the switch.

There's no god anymore, not as he sees it. And karma's a thing that travels both ways in time. He's convinced that the price he's paid for the things he's done gives him a free pass for just about anything. He's a good man, who's made honorable choices. Righteously proud for loving a man who's not worthy of being loved. Who's unloveworthy. So was his relation to the world. Defiantly pushing life up against the wall. It had already killed him. He was shocked to see that it would dare. He counts himself a harbinger and, as such, he was sure that he'd been afforded some protection. To learn of the will inside him, stronger than his will to live, humbled him and tore him to pieces.

"Look at what you did. What have I done? You fucked yourself." When what he really wanted to say but couldn't believe enough to breathe was, *"me, M. You killed me. Me, M. I didn't know. I couldn't have known. You killed me. Now we're both worse than dead."*

Immediately he could see that good and evil don't cancel each other out. They just confound when they coincide. As they always will. J had been so busy taking care of M that he didn't even notice his own suicide. So busy stumbling through fairytales in order to be with him. J, to M, was the full benevolence of this universe. Until he saw M's schizophrenia, or his autism, or whatever undiagnosed aberrance made him fascinating, made him brilliant, tint his expression with an unconvincing indifference to J's execution. At which point, J decided to let his absence be a requiem. Because the worst thing you can do, to a person who's alone, is abandon him.

The worst thing you can do, to damn the whole world, is hold your love separate from your hate. And try to stay where your form can't stand without falling. No matter how much you like falling.

"I know I'm different for having known you. I chose to feel your impact. I wish you were here. But now I'm fully alone. Lost deep to the worst of this. So, so are you."

J once had it in him to resonate, to flow like the blood of the human culture. He used to value what his meat could do, what with his water flowing through it. He misses the arrogant feeling that he might serve some purpose. Now he has a hole inside his abdomen. And stuff just keeps pouring out. An idea which is both absurd and irrelevant.

Now that he's been abbreviated, summarized, he can see the entirety of his self and all his life. He can choose, he can refine all that he wants them to remember. So he's writing and rewriting and rewriting this book. For something solid to hold onto, while the sea reclaims him, as the virii spawn. There's not much time. Unless, so removed from him and it, he might manage something seeming like control. So far, he's failed to control a thing.

So he decides to find a religion.

This is his chaos, the rubble through which he must sift. With one terrible uttering of one screechy word, it all rained down in shards and his time left had been vanquished. He is "reactive," equal and opposite to something catastrophic. On the floor lies every moment that would be his life. He can see them all quite clearly. And the only thing of any importance anymore is the story he can make, the one he'll make them take forward for him, from pieces that no longer add up to a man.

It's the only way, as he sees it, to budge something that's stopped moving. His line, that is. The emptiness in his abdomen has become a fixed point. It opposes every one of his efforts to forward. Even though his miseries, and all they imply, have taught him to dance like a nymph. Strange what you find in your search for abandon, who you'll meet along the way and what they'll teach you about what you've left behind. It's really only an effort to get closer to the pixies so he can steal a handful of their dust. Some parts of him still believe that he might still make it all alright.

Though his time would be better spent riding the flows of this earth. He's already begun by working within the rhythms of the confines of his meats. Next should come the surge of the oceans. Followed by a soar through the air. In high hopes that it'll teach him something strong his will might bend, carry past him into the hastening ether.

3. May 19th, 2007. The life of a man is a series of patterns unfolding. It's the thing, inside the man, observing the physics of a different thing expanding. From a place darker than this, one colder, one without echoes or shelter or hope, something, formerly one thing, chose to see what it might be like to be us all. When existence became a possibility, all those things that did not exist jumped at the chance.

It's the regret of choosing experience over unity that chopped wholeness into packets and keeps it apart. So bear witness, so long as you are, trapped in what flows to where it's all collected.

J went limp.

To resist inevitability is to stiffen its regard. Is to pull down on top of you what you might've gently climbed and stood atop, so that you might've seen for miles. Instead, J had kneeled under the weight of another boy's things crashing down. And he was buried too. This wasn't his heresy. It was that he'd dared look his gods in the eye before collapsing. So came his doom on the 19th day, in the month of May, of the year 2007.

"It descends. I am beneath it. I am crushed."

M carries a plague. He's infested by a million little monsters who've defined him for years, intent little creatures making it harder and harder for him not to rot. He's dying alone in quarantine. A sad lonely frightened boy since before J ever met him through words he'd left on a page. Long before he stopped using words altogether after seeing what another sad lonely frightened boy might do by incanting. By daring to imagine a romance on top of an already buried boy. Burying him irretrievably even deeper.

As the earth spins through an empty infinity, these two are of no significance at all. Neither is the horror that drew them together. Then glued them together. Then ripped them apart. Nor is the shame of loving each other at all. Or failing to. This story holds no truth about two brothers playing men. J will, or has already, bound the word meaningless between them. At most, this is the equating of the spheres in hopes of finding god. It doesn't matter. Not to anyone but them. Each is alone. Together. And their story is your story, is the story of us all. It's what they'll bring back with them when they rejoin what they never should've parted.

Staring at each other, they cannot sense past the nonsense they've concocted. And the balance of inside and out is too treacherous an art not to maintain. As dangerous as a sense of self without context or a sense of the world without perspective. Man's only purpose is to sense and relay. Any interpretation of those senses is an abomination. As is any experience untold.

The pattern is everywhere. Repeating. And some lines, once crossed, trip wires. Then it's a race to choose a side before the trap fully closes. When there's a wall between two people, one must be inside and one must necessarily be out. Unless one of them can find a door or a window or a way to somehow exist between two places.

J's the one who might manage the balance. Even though his history is the uglier one because of the height of the grace from which he fell. He knows that he's killed himself. Well... that he couldn't resist himself being killed. He's become keenly aware that his is not the only will involved in the unfolding of all of this. Though he could do nothing to stop the tumbling. The same way he's forgiven every one of M's transgressions.

What he knows, enough to tell, about control and men's hearts, will chill you.

He can tell stories about M's problems. Reveal the leper or the saint attending him. He can paint a portrait of himself as a hero. Play the victim, play the martyr. Just a child still, playing. Regressing. Deciding men's things. Hurling his will around like a wrecking ball. But that's only happenstance to a greater tale. The real story belongs to the only one who can tell it...

M, the only one who J would be with, is terminally alone. His story will reach no one since words betray him. He's no more than a specter amongst men. When something's moved on its own, or a pale shadow's on a wall, he's usually the reason. He adds mystery to men's lives. Which some men can turn into magic. And no man can be trusted with that.

"He killed me. What more is there? I love him more than I love my own life… apparently. I see that in retrospect. Because he's not alright, I'm not alright. Everything I did to be with him has ended in us apart."

Men bring to them what they dread being near and push away what they most wish next to them. These two are no different. J misses who M never was. He's the only man he's ever loved. The last time they met, six years into it, J kept thinking that M looked so much like someone he used to know. Funny how we all look like someone else. Still, he felt like he knew him. But he wasn't sure. He couldn't reconstruct love with the pieces he had left. Everything came out cockeyed or foundationless.

Since that fateful day, in the month of May, when a little red blotch, and a pain in his crotch, got explained as him wished away. That was the day it ended. The day the veils thickened. When his eyes could no longer see in both directions. And none could see his way. Even as it rippled. As his glands grew stiff and stuck like lumps from his thinning skin. To his terror, he knew he was alone, immediately. With the disgrace he would never be able to explain away. And the death he'd flung at all those who love him.

Now J carries a plague. It makes him like vermin. Which might not be so bad if those romantic parts of his dejected mind could actually manage to believe the notion that he'd taken into him all of his lover's pain. But he didn't take it all. He really only doubled it, at the very least. Now he's alone, foraging for scraps of life, as the latest spawn of M's bloodline. Surely not the only. M spent a year in prison for the birth of all J's brothers. As J waited.

So there are others out there just like him. Bound on all sides by a silence of self, and fits of intellect, having been made acutely aware of the immeasurable distance between them.

Maybe he should've known, never dared a defiant will on the 19th day, in the month of May, the year 2007, knowing what he's allowed be done to his mind. How it searches for messages in sunlight reflected off of wave tips. How it scatters things like numbers and time.

To the crazy stupid parts that were him, that were them, 19+2+7=28. 2+8=10, which is the month of his birth, 19+2-7=14, the day. 2x8=16, the day his lover was born, 8/2=4, the month. They're all bound up in the combination of two and the lemniscate. Just as October minus May is 5. The number 5 has always reminded him of 3 and 2, 32, the year he's always uneasily assumed would be his last. Which is not something that he would ever write down for fear that it would come true. Like everything else he's ever written. Unless he thought that he had it in him to change it.

Sitting in a Montreal café, on the 14th day of October 2007, J finally has clarity enough to write about what's happening to him. It's his 32nd birthday and his blank black sketchbook is full of scribbles now. Things etched illegibly, to be deciphered later, on bumpy roads through a haze of dirt and smoke and dust from ontop rickety old ladders he's had to climb to find books on high shelves where they'd been stored until he could get to them, to figure, to research, to remember any way out.

At this point, he's left all his baggage behind. Somehow, in some mindless way, he managed to let go of the taut life stretching him, straining him to keep it all together, and he just let it all tear apart. It wasn't until he unclenched every one of his flexing muscles that he could see the mess he'd become.

When he finally has perspective enough to begin to relay, he's already weeks into his wander. He's ditched the two heaviest things he's been carrying for so long, his dog and M, weak needy burdens unable to tend to their own. They were his own, his coven, him tending, but he had to leave them lest the story get in the way of its telling. Now he's three times lighter. And the floating strangers he's meeting on his journey are markers of his ascending.

He takes some solace in knowing that he can only fall as far as the forty-year-old woman at the rave who felt the hollowness in his heart. After ricocheting, as if he could, off the beautiful blond boy who said, "wow" when J told him what he's doing as he rubbed his body into a soft sighing slumber. Or the familiar in the strangest strangers. Eyes he's met in dark alleyways.

Beats the days before. After the days after. Once he knew that it could never be the same again. Tiny things insistently revealing that his days are not the same. A papercut at work bleeds into the open air. A drop of blood on the paper. Not until his coworker asks him what's wrong does he realize that he hasn't moved in an hour. Or that wholesome moment when an innocent requests, his two-year-old nephew asks for a drink of his juice. Without so much as thought, even the slightest chance is too much so he pulls away. "Are you clean?" When his hand gets eager, takes cues from a kiss and the eyes of a newfound lover. "No," he has to say, "no, I'm not." He doesn't say, "I'm dirty," but it's implied. He can't say anything. To say anything would be to dare a defense against a persecuting vernacular. He knows he has no right.

He's suddenly the dirty minority. And he's the only one. So it seems… what with the rest of them hiding. As he's hiding. Stupid careless dirty heathen fools. He takes it all as part of his sentence. It can't be more clear than that. Now he's certain, as maybe he was all along, that his ability to love is diseased.

4. Into the night. Into the night, J wanders, where men have rights to their lives and proud claim to their compulsions. Claim abandon to the things they cannot resist. Abandon, to what they'd normally adhere. While the eyes of the waking world are dreaming.

It's easy to wander at night if you're not afraid. Even more so if you are. Guided by it. For this, above all else, J hates M. His easy choice to make no choices. The ease with which he bends to the world.

The places your eyes will lead you in any nighttime follow an unbending will directly. To heed a compulsion's call is to easily wreck your ship on the shoreline. But J doesn't believe in time anymore. He doesn't get to have children so he believes this moment is finally about him. His legacy is not one of bloodlines. His blood has been replaced by M's blood. In no uncertain terms, they are blood brothers. Imagine the romance he's having with that.

Whatever ancestry he might initiate will be a consentless imposition. One that spreads. Unless, like his sire, he chooses to refuse to make that choice. If the choice is even his to make. J sees only patterns in a fractal world. He traces edges always keenly aware of the figure he's defining. He's viral. The only thing that viruses do is reproduce. In this case, through men reproducing. Which is such a silly thought and the reason why the first place he runs, mindlessly after finding out that he's died, is to be fucked by a stranger in a bathhouse. Later he realizes the horror of that compulsion and sees now that he's inclined to infect. Suddenly turned on by every consequence, he's by a million unbending wills directed.

It's the same old story, only his version must be wickedly incanted lest the whims of all these unbending wills still direct him. But they're not really wills, now are they? They're a million little purposed machines, executing. A million little willless vectors intending what he thinks he might control. Which is slightly askew from his "tuck and roll" approach to everything else. But this is his time of desire and he's clever enough to note that "will" can mean "to impose" as much as it can mean "to be disposed."

He thinks he can begin to nurture a glowing sphere inside his empty abdomen. Hoping it might somehow pass for will before it's all over. He thinks he feels a spark in this, his time of genesis, and he wants to see. What's more, he's nearly convinced that he might manage it. When he's fully convinced, he'll start to try. Until then, he depends on the sun.

This is the most pivotally important potent time of his living. Now that he's whittled the external wills down to a few immediate ones that he thinks he might be stronger than. Need has failed to do anything but reduce him. What need defines is little more than lacking. What want defines is a million suctioned tentacles unfurling. J wants M.

Desire is the cause of all suffering but cause and effect get all twisted up in a timeless world of events well predirected. J figures there's something to the logic that he's somehow ended up all alone with all of the suffering so he might as well get what he wants. He's as arrogant as the rest of them when it comes to this. Driven by a growing awareness of a world he's slowly becoming more certain he's created.

As he reconstructs his path, he sees unmistakable patterns evolving. Two years ago, J climbed a cliff from which he was afraid to fall. He jumped from its face as other parts of him debated. He has the power to be mindless when his minds get in the way. This should scare you. A talent of shifting between any of the three people involved in seeing oneself debate oneself.

He didn't make the jump. That would've been stupid. He knew he couldn't make it but it happened anyway. It was the consentless choice of one of the people in between him. He shattered his heels on a rock shelf and had to yell across the lake for help. After JFKing a cotton ball of flesh back into his foot, he started to swim. He watched his friend run along the shoreline to get the boat but J knew that he wouldn't be able to start it. And he couldn't. The hose from the gas tank was cut off. This déjà-vu enraged him, this clarity despite time. He cursed himself for having known all along, as his clean blood drained away and fishes laid eggs and larvae, *"you stupid fuck! You knew this was going to happen."* As though he might've had some choice in what the moment would become.

A déjà-vu is the momentary discrepancy before the coinciding of awareness with experience. It simply means that you're right on track.

In the same way, J loves M, all toxic and impending. With the same mindless abandon, the same leap to faith, the same oblivion to his certainty of outcome, the same exchange of bloods. The sun worshipper doesn't turn a blind eye, he chooses to burn out his retinas because he believes more strongly in other senses. J's still the same boy who used to call to UFOs, the teenager who searched nighttimes for vampires. He's nowhere near convinced, not when it's all as obvious as it is, that it wasn't his damnedest will to end up here all along.

So he's here. There's no other place that he wants to be but there is someone he'd like to be there with him. Which is more information than his sentence relays. So he's saved some time and perfectly placed one more piece. His uncovering of layers consoles him. Maybe, this time, his time is well directed but he's nervous because it pretends a sort of control.

The last time he thought about taking control, abandoned by M, clenched muscles trembling, he found himself wondering whether or not he'd fed the dog enough. About the chicken bones in the fridge. Or if he'd left the fridge door open. Which is clearly not control. Later he would cry about it with the kind lady who was better than him at caring for things. The one who took care of his dog while he could not care anymore for anything and went away to wander. The same one he would later beseech and go unanswered.

He's screaming but no one can hear him. This is his truth to decipher and their wills will only confound. It's a silent prison self-imposed by a man whose skill is telling, whose drive is to explain. Who's swallowed even the possibility of speaking a word of this so that he might pretend a purity and intend an intensity to a problem that the world would lovingly try to take away. Even M has told him to talk to someone in a teary bloody phone call from somewhere far away. To J's absolute fury. That he would pretend to recognize a problem that only he can rectify, but cannot. Will not. For whatever psychotic reason.

For whatever psychotic reason, J believes that M can save him. That loving a man who he refers to as "Agony's Herald" can save him. If he can remember how. He tells a German hard-body named Wilhelm, in a throbbing darklit nightclub, that M has destroyed him. "In other word," the German says in spotty English, "if that means you destroy him too." To which J says, "possibly," he considers and goes on, "if it can be said that two men might share a ruin." He remembers the Mayan phoenix tattooed between M's shoulder blades but doesn't mention it. He thinks of Babylon. They play "truth or dare" at Wilhelm's request. J warns him that he's clever with his truths and foolish with his dares and that, either way, he's in danger.

Everyday J's hand smells like a different man. He misses M. Misses him with whatever he's mindlessly aiming. Starting not to care who he hits. As his disease tries to define him, though his disease is really only a symptom of something slightly worse. As he tries to defy. He resorts and renames, rescinds and refigures. While longing ceaselessly for what he feels he's mostly lost. A conclusion he cannot reach to touch. Bodies have become the direction of his wander instead of places. Just anyone to fucking hold him through all this thrashing. That way, he might not be so lost anymore.

He knows that bodies are not to be trusted. They make us think things with tricky chemicals inspired by memories and forgotten things. But bodies together absolve each other of the need to be more clever. Together, they have it in them to know abandon. Within the negation of duality is all of birth, life and death. It is the only thing.

Luring, like the beacon light in a dark dingy strip bar revealed by the pole, on the stage, aglow from the friction of a cheetah prowling. Ariel has M's body. He's a brilliant redhead with pasty white soft skin and a dick like that. J has an indomitable will toward what people in the past have known well enough to burn. Ariel sees it in J's eyes. He crawls over three tables, kicks a chair into the aisle and lilypads his way over to lick J's face. J follows him later when he goes outside for a smoke. He finds out that Ariel speaks mostly French and that he's auditioning for Cirque de Soleil. He's six months sober, says a bobble on his keychain, bisexual and dating some girl. He's a man. And they have found real life in each other this night. Before the night ends, J pays Ariel ten dollars for a lapdance. Licks him back, kisses his neck, calls him "magnifique," and tells him that he can change the world. Ariel asks J to stop biting.

If it isn't already obvious, J's horrible at the things he's good at. He goes about his time trying to fill holes with holes, believing that entireties must necessarily consist of things that balance and thereby annihilate. He's comfortable dealing in cycling oblivions as they seem consequenceless. Still, these empty brilliant moments always leave him wanting. Which clearly defines having once had something that's gone now. Either way, maybe it's only the cycle that's of any importance to him anymore. Trying anyway to replace what he believes irreplaceable. Really only fueling a fire that won't stop raging.

M's an Aries, a fire sign. J's an ungrounded Libra who can't get enough water.

5. I'm screaming and no one can hear me.

J: Hello.

R: Hey. How's it going?

J: It goes well.

R: Right on. How's the day been so far?

J: Just okay. How's yours?

R: Okay.

J: What are you doing with your time?

R: Not much right now. Putting off a lot of work for the most part.

J: Same here.

R: Feels good, doesn't it?

J: I should do more.

R: Should should should.

J: I'm turning my life into a story so there's some compromise between living it and writing about it.

R: Ha, where's the line? Experience, does it make truth, or just beliefs? Do beliefs limit human experience? If I believe something, does that mean that, right away, I say "no" to fifty percent of possibility? How, then, can I have a truthful experience? Sorry, I guess I'm in a rant kind of mood.

J: Sexy. Objectivity is not something a perspectived creature should seek.

R: Clearly. We prefer the duality. The paradox. Fuck admitting that, hey, maybe this universe is just really fucking strange.

J: As strange as it seems.

R: True enough.

J: So why are you so clever?

R: Or am I just really stupid? Asking questions does not you clever make.

J: Everything is defined by its opposite... they share a border.

R: Are you trying to tell me that I should just fuck roles? Cause, I guess that's what I think of when the talk of opposites emerges.

J: More --- beware implications.

R: Implications structure fact. Variables that we think, think remain constant. They don't.

J: Existence is solid.

R: Existence is fluid.

J: Solids just flow more slowly. That's why enlightenment is freedom.

R: Fluidity isn't linear.

J: Turbulence follows laws.

R: Chaos doesn't. Turbulence is the tension when there are laws.

J: Chaos is defined by man's inability to explain it.

R: Turbulence is defined by man's attempt to.

J: Man is made of meat....

R: ...and water. Can't forget the water.

J: Water is the soul of all life. First flows the water, then beats the heart.

R: Water conducts energy. Energy is the soul of life. Humans retain energy.

J: Water is just what hydrogen can do. Hydrogen is just the balance of positive and not positive.

R: Regardless, H_2O is pretty much me, here and now.

J: If you were in this room, I would breathe your breath and then I guess I would be you too.

R: Yep, you would. And I would be you. But I think I am you.

J: Should I dare kiss you, we might not remember who is who.

R: Sometimes, even death. But birth/death, one and one.

J: I died five months ago.

R: Really? Well, I'm dying right now.

J: Race you.

J: This is like sex to me.

R: This is the kind of sex that makes universes.

J: Universes are an abomination. Selfish curious spirits caged in animals. So silly as to think it might be a fun ride.

R: It's not selfish. If it's all one thing, there's no one to be better than. So silly to think it couldn't be a fun ride!

J: What sort of god would put a man in a cage with an animal that vicious?

R: Ha, what sort of animal would not realize that he and god are one and one? What cage?

J: The meat.

YOU HAVE BEEN TEMPORARILY DISCONNECTED.

YOU HAVE BEEN RECONNECTED.

J: Sorry. Got disconnected.

R: Happens.

J: Tell me your name before they intervene again. Je m'appelle JD.

R: Ryan.

J: I've known two Ryans.

R: Well, I'm Oryan.

J: Then you belong to the sky.

O: A trinity. Remove the split. Be the border.

J: Walking a line is dangerous for a Libra.

O: Not when you're a Gemini.

J: Twins and scales. We are similar. Can I put your words in my novel?

O: What genre?

J: Revelatory.

O: Fiction or not?

J: Ultra.

O: You can quote me. I write as well. Exercise hell. Makes me feel better.

J: I have to write to save my life. I left work. Left Sudbury. Left the story so that it wouldn't get in the way of its telling... now I'm sorting it out. I cry a great deal.

O: It's telling. I promise, it's just about experience. It's not about being here or there. It's about wanting to believe. And then holding on. Surrender control. It's the opposite of giving up.

J: You are brilliant...

O: Surrender allows for an all-around synchronicity and magic. When you hold on, it makes walls, dread, sickness.

J: Synchronicity is two things distinctly pretending one. The word is sharp and has bites. I prefer harmony.

O: You, you hold your hand shut, how will I pass you something?

J: My arms are open. Put it in my pocket... I'll find it later. Just show me.

O: But how will you feel it?

J: Hold it as I walk beside you. My brain extends to the tips of my fingers.

O: Oh, you can look. You can hear. But you won't know, till you handle.

J: Then you'll have to hold on to what I cannot let go... just for a moment. Don't lose it.... and make sure you give it back.

O: Sure, pass it off.

J: I would hate to burden you with it.

O: Shake it out. You won't burden me. Because I let go.

J: You must promise not to lose these things I cling to. They're not solved yet and they are pieces to what might make me whole.

O: Solve? Solve what? Does illumination ask for its pieces back?

J: Yes. It changes their nature when it finds out that we've taken them.

O: Taken. You can't take what's yours. Gotta run.

J: Dinner?

   6. This is how it's going. He's got shards in his fingertips from piecing it all together. Now, like a savant, staring into something crystalline, he's awed. In a good way, but only by contrast. The clearer the picture becomes, the more J sees how it could be more interesting. The more he's motivated toward the parts of the crystal sparkling with the sun. He's having brilliant inspired adventures and realizing himself in glorious ways. Realizing the conflicts and having them out. Some, he pits in fatal duels. Others, he accepts as equal and irresolvable. Those he accommodates.

Then comes the will of the detail that adds itself. There's more to the story by the 27th day, the month of his birth, 2007. A day to balance a year. It's the secular Hallowe'en. R's a punk rock ninja with the ability to disarm. J's unraveling and granting wishes. He tells people to word them well and that there'll be consequences. R's the only one who takes him up on his offer. He's the only one to brave the disclaimer. He must be a fool.

Through two pretend faces, on a day pretending another, through two eager layers of skin, R somehow takes it all away. J didn't believe it could ever really go. Not for long anyway. So he starts counting the days. R's four days old when J writes this, hoping that the one who takes it away's not the one who's left to contend with it.

Everyone has tried to take it away. It's the most recent evolution of mankind: The development of cultural instincts. Everyone knows when you're lying. Or simply omitting a truth. Or not seeing one. And the stakes are higher now, culturally, that's why J hasn't let anyone in. They already know anyway. At some point, every one of his friends has asked him if he's alright. Every one has asked him if he's sick. Which he's not. Or, if he's healthy. Which he is. They all assume which mistake he's made when he makes it obvious that he's been mistaken but will go no further.

He's not alright. But, now, it's only by contrast. The drop of black that greys the white. J sees himself as impure. As having been made impure. Something he couldn't have stopped even if he'd been able to see it at the time. He tries to understand why a spirit, after seeing his path drawn timelessly across the possibility of all being, would choose to inhabit all it entails. He's trying to construct the framework of whatever draw might seduce across realities enough to lure the immaterial into being. He wants to be worthy of being. He feels he can be worthy of being.

Now, what with all his contagion, he has every reason to do what he should've been doing all along. If that's the kind of motivation you need to fully live your life then, like him, you deserve to die. You need to. This is what he's saying to everyone. He's trying to make significant contributions to the lives of the people he meets. It's his new imperative. Not to regain his own purity, that's not possible, but to show them that they must cherish their own. As penance for what he's done. He finally believes in what he can do with his life. And he's living genuinely for the first time.

J believes this is how R was conjured.

When he was in Montreal, if he wrote something good in a day, it was the same as kissing a beautiful boy. Making a friend. Dancing the night away. Figuring something out. Every one of these was equal in intensity and would fill a day. Which explains the sort of mess he's inclined to be in. Each of these things is only part of what it's like for him to love. With M, he had to pour out his own life in order to survive the flooding of overfull days. Floating for so long now in a teacup on an ocean.

He might always be holding out for the someday when M will make amends for the terrible things J allowed him do. Which is the calculated introduction of an equation of proportions by a man who was born in the fall. All the reason why he would not only bear the scathing apocalypse but pull it down crashing on top of him.

He hates the M who keeps him from the M whom he would love, whom he's starting to hate as well. For not being strong enough. For not being able to change. Especially when there's no greater change that J could've made for him. He gave everything to be with him. All he has left are the things that he has no right to give. Like his place in other peoples' lives. Therein must be some refuge. Should he be able to find it. Or have it saunter into his life sporting black tights and a mohawk, always greeted with friendly screams.

The clouds gather into godforms. The setting sun leaves blue streaks inside J's eyes. The blue's not something sensed. It's the memory of creation. He's beginning to see blue light underneath the world, wondering what else his eyes might have recorded and how vivid the images might be. He doesn't believe his eyes. No matter how convincing they are. They eclipse other senses and he's not going that way, searching for what he's searching for. Though it worries him. All these new senses dawning. Just as he finds he has a new sense of emotion. Some new ability bridging the distance between him and the consequences of him, making it alright if he doesn't move.

He saw the same distance carry M away until he was no longer able to accommodate personae outside himself. Humans became only objects to him, deserving no more attention than it takes to turn the knob in order to get through a door. Because of it, M's lost what he loves the most. His ability to connect with people. Either that's the case or it's just with J. In which case, J probably invoked it upon him. Secure that the curse of one is the curse of them both and that the threefold consequences of black enchantments get obscured in the unraveling. It's blood magic.

He now believes that a man needs to be condemned in order to be saved.

So he condemns himself. Basking foolishly in the light of another. Relying. Inasmuch as he knew he was going to get himself infected, and could do nothing against its will, so too does he know that he's not going to seek treatment. He will not. He will heal. But what worries him most about this vigor and bravado is how truly tired he knows his soul is, what with carrying around all that meat, and what this latest test of faith really means. It's so easy now to submit. To submit again to who he might still be, in ways, who did such horrible things to who he's become. Finally, he's the one with his finger on the switch. Imagine finding that inside you.

But you don't want to hear about that, now do you? You already know all about that. You feel it just like everybody else does. And you're just as tired of it.

R likes the colour yellow. He's all smiley faces and sunshine.

The first time R asks J, "are you positive?" he means to say, "are you sure?" People do that all the time. You might not have noticed. J answers both questions, "I don't have to be positive around you," and goes on to say, "you more than compensate." The second time R asks, J can only answer the debt he's incurred by opening his little black book.

He shakes the whole time, lying across him crying, as R reads his story out loud. For no other reason than he's cold, exothermic, the place from which the heat is leaving. As R finds out everything that he says he's known all along. As do all of J's friends. J hates being cold and wet.

A full chapter ahead of time, a character introduces himself and J sees that he's only willed it nearly. So, there are still other wills involved. Or there are none involved at all. It's unfolding. Either way, his will is clearly imperfect. The story is telling itself again. Which is religious. J jumps back and forth of the plotline. This time, he's a bit behind. Next time, he might be all the wiser.

J met R a few weeks before Hallowe'en. They met unexpectedly through a mutual friend at the café where this story begins. It was one of those days when everyone is brilliant and interesting and happy. Except M, who was also in the café but who didn't say a word or make any effort to join the conversation because he was jealous of it, as he tells J later. There's only one lull in the conversation at which point J asks if they'd like to hear something he's written. "Freedom is a religious word..." is the incantation. He doesn't see it at the time but R will be the one who it summons to set him free. If only for a time. J says something about trying to work the concept of "fucking a baby" into his novel for the power of the image. It goes over pretty much how he expects it will.

When they meet again on the bar night before Hallowe'en, J sees a chance and says hello. R asks about his novel. They spend the night together. And the next nine. By the sixth night, R has taken what J was holding onto. What he needed so much. That thing that amounts to his portable hole, like in the cartoons. That nil place inside his heart or mind wherefrom he's been pulling all the horrors he's neglected, to sort, whereto he lets them loose, to annihilate, once done. J has to get it back or learn that he can live without it and all the crippling stuff he's stuffed away inside.

R's a Capricorn, an Earth sign. J's a newly grounded Libra, tethered but still in flight. In R's presence, J's capable of balance. R gives balance to J. A stable enough lot that the things he builds don't teeter. He's doing something important. But this is the first time he can see it. His extents are quickly exceeding his form and he's no longer sure of what he's capable. He's terrified of structures that keep standing and what sort of world he's inclined to build. Knowing what he fears he's already wrought. Especially when he finds that he's happy now. Underneath it all. Having been buried before.

He tries to explain this to R but how do you explain that what you're doing necessitates that you be insane to a boy who's eight days old? He's the author of his life now. To varying degrees. R just confirms it. J asked the world, "Yo world. Are you for real?" A three-foot tall man, all dressed in green, was the only one in the crowd to stake his shillelagh, jump up, click his heels and yell, "Aye!"

M calls and asks to come home. J searches his pain and his triumph, his options, his heart and his soul. He tells M to stay away. He knows it will be the same. And that's the opposite of progress. The opposite of what's making him healthy. It's time to be happy now. The story demands it. Even if he feels so unsure. So he chooses himself. And M's no part of him. You see? M wants to come home. J's no home to him. Not now. The time came. As the time always comes. And J and M were not equals. The imperative was not achieved and it has changed now.

"Search for it, man, I'm no part of you either."

The story hasn't started yet. Ways have only been made for it to happen. J doesn't know where to begin. He ends up at K's house. He needs her help and can finally ask for it. She's a friend who knows him on the only level he accepts to exist. Through his writing. The same dark woods he braved to find his way to M. He hands her ten thousand words of a manuscript. She's reading this right now. So is R. They look up. The moment they share is simultaneous.

Look up. It's all around you.

7. No, seriously. A man's morality is a fixed point around which his psyche revolves. It's an emergent pattern in the nonsense, existing outside of his ability to affect it. The average of the horrors done to him and those he's done in return. A man's spirituality is the opposite of that. It doesn't pertain to the meat. Or to any of the meat that surrounds him. It's the substrate from which the meat condenses. It's seeing a picture of old friends at a party and realizing that one of them's now dead.

It's not alright that things should be suddenly different. Things keep getting dramatically radically suddenly different. Quickly enough for J to note what's not changing. Anything solid in the river rushing by. Some jagged thing he might hold onto. He worries that he's still just tumbling. He now believes that his words cause synaptic patterns in the brain to fire and overlap, creating electromagnetic fields resembling snowflakes in the sun. Depending upon your perspective, this is, at once, the most beautiful thing and the most terrifying.

So he dawns a cloak and goes wandering in familiar crowds. Enticed by the truths he can scavenge then rearrange. He's vampiric with it, lost to the romance of beautiful boys, dark nights and bloodfeeders. Which means that he's still not in control. He worries that he'll always be patterned and crystalline like all the love he's ever managed. He's understandably restrained, unsure what any of it intends, certain he's not the one intending it.

Most of the time.

He's been led to frightening places in the past, scary things revealed, lurking in the dark, along the way. Love, for him, is akin to abandon. It's wandering barefoot through the dark woods at night. The total submission of a man's undirected all given to unskilled hands to wield. It's what it takes to trust someone entirely with your identity.

Inasmuch as love renders the lover powerless by redoubling his capacities and obscuring his limitations, intent on carrying him away, so too is there a place, akin to love, wherein a man might be offered a chance. That moment before an act of grace is bestowed, or an atrocity committed, in which a man's truly alone with himself, unpatterned by the eyes of the world. Within this moment, he has threefold clarity. There can be no doubting this or lying about it. Abandon is always a choice. Which marks it as hypocrisy. One that arises only after all other choices have been wished away.

To commit to abandon is unclearly one of two things: It's either to forego one's role in an unfolding reality or to assume it wholly. The former demands a refined definition of the concept of will. The latter, of soul. Neither of which J holds or believes useful. He searches for simpler parallels to the things he can't understand. And the gods are both appeased and honored.

When J left home, all those months ago, a lady with a crooked eye gave him an Inukshuk talisman. She's a sad but feisty gal with a heart as strong as her will. Not so strange that she should see him clearly. The dust had long-settled on her disasters so she could recognize his just rising. He treated her gift very seriously. When you approach someone as an oracle you must take what they say for prophecy. She left him with an obligation. To leave word in the places he would wander to direct those who would follow his way. He's called himself "harbinger" for years but only now believes he's nearing something worth saying.

He's trying to make a very specific sense of things. Which is a threat he's found inside him. It promises to make him a liar, a betrayer and someone not to be trusted. Understand, a fear mechanism has been triggered and primal instincts have kicked in. Fear used to compel him. It's not so strange that it should also impel. A fog has settled overtop his clarity and obscured every horizon. He's searching through the mist but can find no landmarks to guide him. Other than an obvious sense of something ominous. He has every direction in which to walk but no clear idea where any path might lead.

He'd almost fully mapped the labyrinth of pathways and corridors with such fine detail. Then R came along and shook his Etch-A-Sketch. Now there's just a startled Minotaur sitting on a toilet, reading Vanity Fair. J's making efforts to overlook how ridiculous it is. Fully aware that horns still puncture lungs and that it's just the two of them anymore. Always him and a horned thing and an etiquette to be maintained.

There are times when he catches it lurking. In places he's a pervert to have looked. In the strange sadness on R's face the first time J gulped down his cum. Like a seagull swallowing a fish. Without hesitation or consideration. Which seems like certainty to some. Or the uncertain terror in R's eyes, staring at his hand, the first time he wipes J's tainted cum off, across his panting belly. Or in the slowing of their rhythm when the sex gets only so hot. When the cum starts to boil then no more. Feeling certain sin and blasphemy in the sacrilege of holding back a geyser. And awaiting punishment. Aware that heat will melt rubber and that they need rubber between them at all times. Or when R gets too randy and bashes teeth against lip to bloody it. Then the moment when they realize, when they make real, that they cannot exchange waters. Which makes things difficult, since they're both biters, who like to drink, but only one of them better bleed.

Clarity is the opposite of abandon. Therefore clarity is the opposite of love.

J's desperate for R to fuck him. To force that ripe thick cock up his tight wet ass. To feel that split, feel it tear, him suddenly deep inside. They roll around, bruising, doing everything for hours, till both of them're raw, but that. But that skewering moment of absolute rapture. All because J fucked it up. That slippery moment of complete surrender. Of Midgaard's kiss. That basest part of his, plunging deep inside the deepest parts of his, and grinding. Pumping till it comes. All blue sparks and lightning between slick tongues entangling. Setting fires. And bolts to thunder. Blazing through men's meats. When they're soaking, pressed to one, heaving oceans comingling. Brains down to the tips of their fingers, clawing. Always only cells apart.

Cells apart.

When R's seventeen days old, he's still powerfully bright and burning but, by this time, J has seen into his dark. Upon meeting, if only in J's mind, this bright, this dark, these two things annihilated to even a dangerous field. In this respite, J cleverly took the chance to learn R's power of disarming. It's a young magic and R couldn't defend against its going. When R noticed the thievery, in cat-like fatality strikes, they disarmed each other. Now they're just two naked guys caught sitting on the toilet, reading Vanity Fair.

That's what you get for messing with simultaneity.

J's desperate to fuck R too. But he could never do that to him. Not in all good conscience. He strips himself of the power to invoke it. He hasn't had his dick inside anything since he found out. Other than M. This is his deepest regret. You have no idea how important it is for him. How he's so easily enthralled in ancient magics. The center of a thousand suctioned tentacles unfurling. No idea how hard it is to resist his urge to allow the snake inside him to swallow its own salts. To breathe through the mouth of another, searching for the gateway woven deep down into forever. That sense of impossibility between two people attempting to unite. Hissing as it tries to fall through the portal, cockbound forever to the hard cock inside, dragging him along. To find some way into right now. And the forevers woven deep down into it.

It's sewn into the way men travel through time. Knowledge is the price they pay, allowing room for only one accumulating moment. A man's awareness of his life depends on him witnessing the ripening of his meat. Awareness is the opposite of knowledge. One meat aging, one man suffering it. Such is the equation. That the awareness of men should smear moments into lives. This is his strongest weakness, burrowing through him as he burrows through time, and the only way that any man might be understood.

J's desperate to fuck R so his only recourse is abandon. And he's already made that choice. Stupid careless dirty heathen fool. Who allows his brain to wander. To that certain moment when an awareness dawns. One desire separated by two layers of skin. When tongues give way to teeth. As flesh rubs raw flesh red. Two hard cocks wrestling between four pounding hips, slick with spit and semen. That bated frenzied moment when R finally answers J's unspeakable pleas and grunts, "I want you to fuck me."

Though J never would. At least not consciously. These are just thoughts. Just thoughts about how he'd do it. How he'd fold his legs back and reach with his tongue to loosen. The smell that lets him froth and frenzy, lingering round his lips. Then let loose a little howl. To the moon and the dark gods hiding round it. Then slick it up and slip it in. Choicelessly. Thoughtlessly. Cravenly slip it in. Slowly slide inside. Safely. Watch his eyes roll subtly back. Enraptured. You have to keep him safe. Have to protect him. From him. And all the evils inside. Rocking them. Up him, through him. He'd fuck him like you'd fuck a baby... if you had to. How you'd gently. How you'd softly. How you'd prayerfully play. Do everything to keep him safe. From all the evil inside.

Ah well, it's for the best, anyway. No one ever forgives you for your illness. So you might as well submit. No one ever ends up loving you for the reason they fell in love. It's best to keep these sorts of things to yourself. Besides, it's true what the cultists say about sexual energy and creative energy. That they're the same thing. Which has great implications and suggests a balance to maintain. You see what it means to him. And what it's done to him. It's the energy it takes to create life. It's blue streaks and sunlight. This is what he's denied. Life inside him has become a threat and its absence has put new instincts into him. It's demanded he become a creature of pure thought. Since that sort of thoughtlessness is no longer a choice. And any real creature of thought knows that his only hope is to become one of will.

It's made him an artist. Taught him that the energy he expends might be generative when instead it could so easily consume. J spends his time trying to learn how to direct it. After seeing how it's inclined to direct itself. Crash him, along with it, tumbling into craggy shorelines.

One fluid, one not.

He's approached it from every angle. Seen the compromise and the conflict as clearly as he might. He sees that he's responsible and that there's no way he could've stopped it. In any case, it's only too late that he's begun to see through time. No matter. A timeless boy knows what it's like to be buried so he can't seriously be afraid of that anymore. And the rotting, either way, is something that he was going to have to endure. Of the endless number it might have been, this is his path to wander.

He's on a bad path and he knows it. But he's a good man.

By this point, M has been wished away. *"I wish him back."* He has the most interesting answers to J's most interesting questions, as J sees it, suggested by the littlest sense he's managed to make.

Clearly, a defenseless boy must be in complete harmony with his environment if he's going to survive. Especially boys who cannot harbor life without dying for it. Thereby, M should be dead. But M's not dead. M clearly knows something that J does not. It's will that's kept him. Somehow. Volatile and disinclined toward the good. No matter. It's will that will keep. What with wills all around. How long could you hold yourself together, knowing that you have to? How long could you stay awake, knowing that, two days after this chapter is written, M will ask J to let him come home again and R will have been inside him?

J's doubly afraid. He always has to compensate for someone else's fear that's not enough. He's been stupid. Sure. He's a smart boy. Of course he's a fucking idiot. Like that artist boy in Montreal who wanted J's fucked up cum all fucked up inside him because he just didn't care anymore. So now J has to care for him as well. Because now J knows better. Every fucking idiot does. He's followed M through the worst of this world. Reconstructed horrors he could barely reenact. Then enacted them. To understand. That no single step need be cautious on a path that's preordained.

He still doesn't understand why he's always the last to know. Why it's always his role to care. Why he can't stop caring either way. Longing for what defines the ends of him. And what exists beyond. Always having to wait for it to be revealed in the eyes of other people. It's the hardest path for a man to walk. One defined by his own limitations. But it's the only one that leads to transcending. It's so easy for J to be with R. There's absolutely no reason to question a thing.

Besides, no one ever really *has* to fuck a baby.

8. This is what he found inside him. He knew as soon as the latest prophet told him not to be scared, that he's already made the choice and simply has to follow through. Even though he's stopped, the rest has kept on moving. The drone of it's resounding. Affecting what he can and cannot do. He was wise to follow his heart as it was compelled to wander into some unremarkable vastness. It made everything that remained so obvious. In a white infinity, across an endless white page, all that remained was his morality. And its consequences.

For simplicity's sake, and to speed things along, he has to choose between two boys. Well, for the sake of self-respect, between what both represent. What shoots off as implication and what ripples the rest of what he does. His novel is what he does. It's his finest masturbation. And what each choice implies decides which story he'll tell. Whose life'll change. And how responsibly.

To not choose is to resist consequence. Is to threaten to unravel a universe woven of cause bound to effect. That's not something he would dare. Though it doesn't matter either way. This must simply go on and he must simply endure it. He can tell that story or he can tell this one. Both of which are parts of what he really wants to say. His hesitation is just him waiting for his will to come to terms with it.

One boy promises twice the world, beyond what he's conceived so far. All its threats and wonders revealed to him in the interim. His timeless purgatory spent exploring the causes he's given his life for. The other offers shelter from that very thing. A chance to construct a fortress around which to build a world. A man in the universe. A universe in the man. There's no overlap or comparison between the two. Except that, only one face on a Russian nesting doll continuum can expect to see the light for very long.

As things become more clear, sitting on the couch in front of the television, high, watching movies and his candle's flicker, he decides the next chapter. Trapped in a town he wants away from, between two men he can't abide, being eaten from the face down. He makes only efforts to remember. Memory, as the only real psychotic event, is the only real key to identity.

He has a toothache. Some innocuous morsel, meant to sustain him, got caught where it shouldn't have gone. Then it started to rot, forcing him into a painful respite. He realizes that his world has gotten messy again. To his terror. It's getting more and more pressing that he learn to manage it. And that he manage it well. Or become able to bear what comes of it. The blue-black scar on his knee from the last time he got all cancerous makes him worry whenever he gets less than well.

M has four giant blue-black scars on his body. Though he wears them better than J does. The first is on the left side of his soft supple ribcage. He told J it was an insect bite. It happened when J was not a part of his life. Anymore than any other time the two have gone their ways. The second is on M's right upper arm. He told J it was a bee sting. He said he pulled out the stinger with his teeth and left half the stinger inside. J wasn't a part of his life for this either. The third is on his right upper thigh. J found it when he leaned in to kiss him and was greeted by a clenched fist and a scream. Then J watched as M surgically attended. He casually stuck a needle in the red-black scab in the middle of the red sore pool swelling up his leg. It bled black blood in a deep dark river for hours. M said it was a bee sting. For god's sake. It happened during another one of the hundred times when J wasn't a part of his life. When J could only witness the insects swarming from afar. The last was on M's left lower calf.

That's not true, the last was just under J's left knee. It was the only time M ever showed J empathy, or understanding, when he held his wounded leg and touched softly enough to touch. J bumped it one day on his jeep and barely even noticed. Didn't even break the skin. Within a week, it was a red lump creeping down his leg. Within two, an alien cigar burn bleeding black blood. Neither M nor J knows what it is or why. Neither's going to ask. M has no words to ask or to share should it come to him. And the last time J had reason to entrust someone with power over his details they took away most of his life.

In some unavoidable retrospect, J reconstructs every moment. All the reasons and the things he did despite them. He remembers drinking M's black blood. All those desperate times. In the memory of every touch, every kiss, every soft embrace, he now feels that shadow condensing between their skins. It only makes sense that he'd be punished for continuing to press. Daring one in a universe that depends wholly on all things opposed to the notion. Where one is to be. And one plus one equals naught.

J prefers caverns to mountaintops. What might wash off of other people, for him, tends to pool. His yoga cult best friend tells him this means that he has an excess of energy that needs to be siphoned off. He's spent his time with M bleeding bright white light from his chest deep down to cure M's darkness, to someway relieve his own. Holding him tight entire nights through, hard against him. Never soaked enough in another's sweaty night. Waking, so often, to lick the water they have between them. Sweat, spit, tears, semen.

Now blood.

Blood magic's a strange magic for creatures whose world is as fluid as it is solid. As much as it holds hope that its vapors might lead up to the sky. It's the same magic J used to see if he was right. The same prayer he prayed when he spat pneumonia into M's mouth before he left him behind that time and headed for Vancouver. M ended up in the emergency room. J just had to know if what he suspected was true. If, without his bright white light being bled deep down into him, M couldn't sustain his own. As it turns out. Not enough to bring him back to life. Not enough to kill him.

"Je ne te soutien encore."

Anyway, J has a toothache. He's now terrified when parts of him swell and ache, knowing now that he's the perfect martyr incubator. And how grandly he can word whichever cause his will might choose to fight for. He's now, quite literally, always fighting off infection. Silly and redundant. And more important than ever to note.

He's failed in the past to, and still cannot yet, harbor life. Microbe, cancer, hope or love. But now he's been made mortally aware and might stand some sort of chance because of it. He knows enough to recognize his last hope. What with all the places M's gone and dragged him. It would disgust you to know where he's been. Mortally aware that, if he lets down his guard, he's gonna sprout like a Chia pet. Unless he can achieve some sort of synchronicity of selves. Some harmonic resonance obscuring the horizon between identity and what identity is made of.

Or what if one of those blue-black scars erupts from the center of his face? The first week he spent alone with this thing, these things that M fucked inside him, he found a lesion on his back. It was really just a scratch from doing crunches on the floor but it takes a second to figure that out. A few minutes if you're fucking hysterical.

Ah, but he's learning. How to become holy. How his glands will swell, stiffen and tender two days before he needs to cry. How his body will tell him exactly how his life is really going when his mind can't find a way. Just as a pain in his tooth told another in his line of prophets about his indecision. J sees that he must learn how to use the fire's light as well as feel its warmth. And whatever other sense might be applicable to a thing that can dance so freely.

When you're human, fire tends to burn if all you do is feel it. Just as any man goes blind when he stares too long at the sun. So J decides to build a pyre. As well, he asks R to dance. Unfamiliar glowing things must be approached from all sides. He knows he has to stop hating M. By understanding that hate and love are not opposites. At most, they're opposite expressions of the same thing. One, the price paid, for one, the deviation ventured. Their opposite is indifference. By understanding that, he might move on. By deciding that someday he will stare at the sun until he's either blind or transcends.

Regardless, he sees that the story is making the choice for him. There's nothing he understands more intimately than this. It's the sway as his ocean swells. It could be that the choice has been made all along, without his knowing, and his story just reveals it. Which is why he's writing it. To make concrete what would exist otherwise as only whispers. A man can only be spared for so long from what he's inclined. He sees that the story's choosing M.

"He has my life. He took it when I gave it to him. He did just what I asked him to do." The worst thing you can do to a person is give them exactly what they want.

Which isn't quite true, beyond an obviously flimsy definition of the word "I." True, M had J's life. Then he gave it away. Now J's life somehow hangs limply from the mouth of a giant cobra. Impaled on one of its fangs. Paralyzed by the venom. He's not sure and the moment requires too much attending for him to skip ahead to figure it out. What he needs is someone who's capable of promises. Someone whose affect on his life will hold. Hold truths from which life will grow. J told M to never let the season change with them still apart. Summer turned to winter before it was realized. The ground is cold now. And nothing will grow in it for months.

Just as winter draws into it the outward look of life, the hand that throws the flame feels only its absence. Water freezes, this time of year, when man's most dependent on fire. In a way, this explains the story's choice. J's keenly aware that he's looking at R through a pair of eyes. At all times, there's flesh between them. R wants J to meet his mother. But J fears, should she truly meet him, she would annihilate. She's his opposite; she gave R life. So the story goes. Just as J sees that M's the figment of an imagination that seems no longer able to conjure him. Which leaves room for possibility again. Now that memory's out of the way.

Once, all they had to do was become equals. Then they became equals and obliterated each other. Seems true that two things equal in size, stature and status should be twice any one alone. But that's just not the case. Unless bound into something greater or sheltered by the same, they must necessarily exist as part of what the other is not. Paradoxically equal and opposite. Therefore, when they meet, they annihilate. Should they not be able to resist the singular will to collide. Which, for a boy groomed on contrast, is the key to all life.

Should he find a way to come to terms with it.

Five years ago, J had a day with a friend. The woman who owns the café in which this story begins. They went together to buy new outfits, changed into them in a grocery store parking lot then went their separate ways. The point was to pretend that ten years had passed, to pretend to meet each other anew and to tell each other stories to catch up. J had been a con artist and a traveler. He'd written a novel and published some articles. His blood was the same color as his blood is now.

Such is the power of words, upon their invocation.

Words are something smeared across states. They exist as pure singular wills, anchored in the real world, chained to things ethereal. Combined, they amplify and confound. They're patterns travelling through the mediums of other things. As the true expression of the ocean is held within the waves. Most of all, they're pleas beseeching. Sadder than a tin can echo resounding. They're one meaning intended between two perspectives. Something like trees in the forest.

Or the unlikely coinciding of disparate things.

But he won't say anything more about that. He knows it's his awareness of those creatures that draws their attention nigh. He sees the messages. And that they're being sent covertly. By one creature, who must be afraid of another, sneaking secret codes that need to be deciphered. So tests are implied. Tests to be passed and characters refined. J's certain only that there are two conflicting wills, or sets of inclinations, intending some series of outcomes of which he might be fit to be a part. At this point, it remains unclear which creature he should trust.

He needs some sort of clearer sign.

When M calls and says, "I miss you," J becomes a blue dragon. Horns and scales rip through his scalp and skin as wings tear free to raise him into the sky. Winds gust dirt storms round. He belches fire when he bellows deep, "You betrayed me in the name of ridiculous things. What kind of man are you? Show yourself."

But it doesn't matter. To find your lover astonishing is to hate him for settling for you. Just as two equal things must obliterate unless singly intended. Just as the concept of obliteration must somehow involve words. As, then, so must to craft its opposite: For two things, doomed to collide, to resist the single will between them, is to connect them to the possibility of all other wills combined.

So I assume.

9. Coming to terms. So I assume. I assume small creatures walking through my brain must feel much like I do in the forest, on a winter's day, with sunlight flashing off snowflakes between the shadows and limbs of bare trees entangling. I wish I could run a needle over the snow dunes, as you can over a record, and have every sparkle of sunlight make a sound. I think their messages would be easier to understand should you be able to hear them sung to you.

Winter draws the life from living things back into the solid earth. A clever man, or one desperate enough, might learn to sense direction from it. Whenever there's a flow, there's a source and a sink and a reason why for the spiral. In a way, J's glad to have staked the vector of his life from choice to consequence. Or to have had it done to him. Should he manifest the stamina, or muster the courage, he has a chance now. He can move laterally. He can orbit spirally about his path, sweeping tenfold the field a hastier man might pass. Find merriment while dancing to unravel the maypole.

It comes to him in wisps of answers on the wind.

He sees white fire when he holds his hand against the still blue snow. In a moment of curiosity, he follows its fluttering. He turns to find himself engulfed in flames. He sees that they're white flames so he feels no sorrow. He's been taught something. The hand that throws the heat feels only its absence. And the loss of whatever fuel's burned away.

Within all living creatures is a will toward life. No matter how absurdly that life is lived. As in all things whatsoever there's a will to simply be. These are the hands at his back. These are awarenesses, not knowledge, you either have them or you don't. You can either use them or you can't. Like the immense power that some men feel affecting their lives. The intense pressing down, changing them.

They're primordial with it.

J used to leap through the air in his dreams though he never really managed to fly. Always scraping his face on the roadside or sliding down the side of a wall. Until he learned to brace himself against the impact. Floating, before hitting, on waves shot forth from his hands. On the first winter day, he nearly hit a rock-cut on his drive home. In his mind, this is all that saved him. His father said god was with him. Sometimes.

Othertimes, a man's left alone to consider what's been done. Things he cannot help but see. Beyond all sense of ego and involvement, there's a nil place where choice and consequence unfold and reveal a stranger place in which a man might choose to take responsibility for the world as his own flawed creation. This is a pivotal moment in which a man chooses between sanities. Depending upon the world he wakes to find round him. Then comes the guilt. The shame. The absolute sense of failure. Unless he's dreamed the sense of his own discord. Which few men ever do. What, with so many wills slithering all around. So it falls to the overwhelming sense of the importance of understanding the harmony that flows between people. And what such a flow might do. What affects men have on other men's lives.

Standing in a crowd has become like cold ocean water rising round a man chained to the sea floor. He feels the water on his jaw and can no longer be unsure. So the sway of the moon must be trusted as the reflection of the sun. Which a wise man knows connects him to all of creation. Right down to the affects their wills have on his life.

Now J can't help but feel them. The first time it happened, he boiled up with cold sweats and tremors and had to run away. It happened right after he realized what he'd been searching for and why he could never find it. A man in the universe. A universe in the man. That there's greater sense to be made of what he's been feeling all along.

It was at a bar. He looked out over the crowd, at all the faces he knew, knew him, and he felt what it meant for them to be part of his life. What hold they held over who he might be. The nausea sent him tripping from the room, through the nearest door or whatever portal to wherever. He ended up in the washroom, staring into the mirror. Talking to himself about who he might be. And what he might hold onto in the deluge. Just like M used to do.

Just like M used to spend hours in front of his own eyes, as an oasis, amongst a desert of a thousand not his own. Then J understood. Brought to him by the force of a thousand wills pressing. Pushing him toward the only one. The only one there is. Suddenly his equal. His opposite. The reason for all of this. Explained in a world made of light.

It's now clear to him that there exists some line across which they are mirror images. Where right is a matter of perspective, clearly deciding what's left. For two things, doomed to collide, to resist the single will between them is to connect them to the possibility of all other wills combined. As to follow the forces all pressing down is to find the way back to from where you've strayed. Then it's either crash clumsily or bow gracefully and begin to orbit.

Let the stars be our guides.

J runs through scenarios in his mind about ending it with R. He doesn't want to end it with R. He needs a friend and someone to touch him. But he has to give R the chance to make that choice too. Considering what's really going on. This story's about what prices and stakes it means to be with M. Only through R did he realize it. To a clever boy, every aspect of a perfect distraction hints at something powerfully missing. He picks one of the truths and tells R that it's over. He's not distracting anymore. He's the opposite of distracting. He's one fuck away from being the worst reality J can imagine. Which he realizes, as he writes it, is M's reality.

But that's too much for him to consider. So back to it.

J wants a different M. One this M has proven himself incapable of. One J's novel, his whole work of art, is intended to incant. Or to explain. Or whatever other dimensions might be merged into an insufficiently dimensioned thing to make it okay. These are the things inside him, explaining why there are all these other things inside him. Why it's best he be left alone in front of mirrors outside crowded rooms. Where he found M again. Through the deepest and the darkest, the utmost worst he could bear. And will have to.

J's the only one who had it in him to find his way into M's world by becoming a specter everywhere else. Just to see how alone he truly is, standing by the mirror. There's no one else. And, with these words, J binds him there. If only to make reason of the violence he befell him. The Fury chose the Fate in these men's lives. The men confused the will to annihilate with the will to unite.

Now every day is just more "without me."

Until he can make it all right. Or remain clearly unable to figure out how he can live with him or how he can, if he must, live without. Now it has to be true. All these fairytales he's always been told and their promises of happy endings. Good always wins over what's not good. That's already in the mass awareness. As soon will be the idea that there's no line to be drawn between a man's choices and the world they make. Once he chooses his perspective. Or deems something worth looking at.

It's his idea of M that keeps him searching made-up memories, real and not. Until sorted, they'll fragment him into all the people he might need to be in order to accommodate whoever else is there with him. He stares at the sun. Into the overlapping brilliance of all the combinations of all the information there ever might be. The unending stream of white fire. He's placed a lens between them. Through which only certain light will pass. Be cleansed and be bent into the perfect image, who'll walk up to J, who's eager to love him again, and allow it.

So goes the manual, intending explanation as incantation, to convince himself of what's going on. Mathematically better-fitting theorems to fully confine what varies. Staring at the sun, searching a million white images for a mind refined enough to see them. Searching to refine one. Going half-blind in one eye to pull a raven from the sky. Realizing that it might take more.

It's difficult but he tries to remember the good. Eclipsed things he hasn't thought about for years, only trusted. It worries him that the thoughts come so slowly. As though, instinctively, he's not ready to forgive. Or to be convinced that there's any way back to the place his true self's been held captive, guarding the last of his love, while false selves have tended to his life.

The first months J and M spent together were the best J's ever known. He was made brilliant by being able to love someone he worshipped. It's the source of the irresistible momentum of his universe expanding regardless of what it's come to contain. He tries to remember what it once meant to believe in someone. And what it means that his love's since been denied.

There was purity once. J assumes.

J remembers, but will not recount, the exact moment when the loss of his innocence began travelling both ways in time, altering his memories and tainting any new ones. Before which his love was idealistic and would've done anything. Before it exhausted itself, doing it all, and was expected to do it again. An unendurable loop unending, jading him further each time round, while the din of time's mockery resounded. Until it stuck.

Time, put simply, is the progression of things. It exists wherever anything learns, grows or changes from what it will never be again into something else. This isn't a will toward death. It's a will toward evolution. The word "love," held up to a mirror, is a sigil for "evolve." So J follows, leaving behind a mind intent on dwelling in caverns without light. The effort demands he think beyond the only things he knows. Dig deep into a stab-wound, long since healed over, and pull out a broken-off piece of blade.

This is no game but it must no less be played. This chapter was supposed to be about remembering the good. But he can't forget enough to remember. So he needs a show of faith.

10. Show of faith. Holding his cock is like holding a weapon. The source of all his mayhem and downfall and why he so easily embraces evil. As running a hand over his porcelain skin is feeling what millions of years of evolving life has intended for you to feel. It places you within the continuum of things that are meant to be. Lets you believe that you too are intended. Lets you feel safe by showing you that there are wills attending.

It's not a matter of faith any longer. Not as the world's been explained. Now it falls to the story and how convincingly it's told. The only difference between belief and knowledge is perspective. We stand as the guardians at the threshold, responsible for the heights, the depths and the impossible rifts between simultaneous worlds that cannot coexist within us. So it tumbles. According to what each might sustain until each might reconcile his own wills of man.

No man is simple but some men will never know it. Some men are aimed toward a purpose, will wander and never waiver. They, as all men, exist as memories do, amongst other things, inside a giant mind. A million years explain them as they are part of what explains a million more. Other men exist between men. They act as nodes to and from which information flows. Through them, mankind is connected and accelerated and shaped by the way they bind. Others, still, exist between worlds. They cannot know the ends of themselves as dreams are what imply. To transcend is their only purpose, then to shine and light the way. They're ultraviolet.

Such is the use of man, which no man, trapped in the flow of it, will ever come to know. All these things repeal when any one of these men stands still. Right down to the marrow of what he believes to be bones. It's then that he sees reason to choose. He walks backward in his own footsteps, retracing wherefrom and why, dragging memory back beyond the point where he fractured. Past his irrelevant failures and ridiculous struggles to a time before consequence delayed...

Holding his cock is like holding a weapon. How it's tapered to a salted point, bulging where you'd grab it to pull it near enough to smell. Ravenous. How it tastes when you try to swallow all of it. How it feels warm against your neck and chest. He's a redhead but not the kind you'd recognize unless you've searched hard enough to find his third nipple. So his shirt's off and you can see that his white skin's soft and smooth and light. He's warm against your chest as you writhe entranced and rub against him. It's sticky between you. Salted like a threshold across which no harm might pass. You've tasted every inch of him. Soaked now, mixing yours with his as plumes of steam rise up around you. You want to drink what comes of him. You want to feel him inside. There's nothing more important than those moments of absolute rapture. When he lets you love him. Love him enough to crawl inside. And him inside you. His size makes you bleed and you pull him deeper. Closer. Call his name.

If you can name it, you can take away its power. Should its name suffice as its explanation. Otherwise, it takes all the words you can utter to make sense of it. To understand why you've borne the crushing weight it's held you under. To finally be able to forgive and see why.

It's impossible, though, to travel both ways in time for a creature whose name must be spoken. To understand consequence, you must first witness what's its cause but to return to a time before something has happened is to negate its ever being. Is to unravel it all to return to a place of likelihoods and possibilities. Maybe, even, to a time when a choice was made and to the chance to make it better.

Or to an awareness of one or the other.

J remembers loving M. He's never forgotten. It's been the source of his onward in the face of blistering winds and hail. All the reason for him to hate in fiery torrents, flooding the worlds he's tried to build with churning rivers of molten lava. Past the boiling oceans and poisoned reservoirs of pooled rains that fell like acid. There's no greater sting than such a thing as such a glorious love denied. Splatters from the bleeding heart of a brilliant man, with another brilliant man designed.

It was M's pain that first drew J. For so long now, he's been unable to not believe this. What he sees in the things he's done, and those things done to him, is just a sad will toward an end. But now he sees that he might reach deeper. He has to take cues from all he's said as he's explored who he's become. Why he's different, without consent, as his story explains itself. He's begun to hear truths within the things he's been listening. He doesn't know what he's talking about but he believes what he's saying. It's still growth, though "growth" is not the right word, when something becomes more intricate.

Some things grow like trees, reaching deeper and higher for their sources of power. Some things grow like cancer. One connects the earth and sky, risking lightning. The other, seeking one pure breath, risks suffocation.

It's raining as J sits outside an emptying dancebar, rocking with his head in his hands. He repeats and mutters all the things he knows. Just to remember, just to be sure. *"If something is true on one level then it must be true on every level and this is the only way man might know god. Every man has whatever he needs within an arm's reach to solve whatever problem he might face. Karma's a thing that travels both ways in time. Men bring to them what they dread being near and push away what they most wish next to them. Man is responsible for everything that happens to him, right down to the rain."* Over and over, but It does no good. Nor hints where any might be uncovered.

What formerly had to be flung, he chooses to direct. He fuses the chain on his wrecking ball and works the muscles he'll need to lift it.

It's love that's fueled his putrid hatred. It's the righteous smiting of those things in the way of the expression of his purest holy. It's the sad fact that the object of his affection is the obstacle objecting, by its nature if not by its choice. Finally, it's come time for him to reconcile his own choices with this fact.

His love cannot exist without the ability to express it and he cannot express it without consent from the one he loves. It's just hatred any other way. No matter why. He must be permitted. There's a will in the way of the expression of his potential. Some shepherd oracle who's able to see beyond who he's already been. Who reached for the extents of him and found that he could not touch. So, instead, he decided to block, to redefine the path that another man must take to be brilliant.

He says its name.

M loves him. J knows it. Like he's loved him all along. Each dragging their hold on the other through what they call lives. Weighted down by it in their horrible absences. All knotted up when standing side by side. The more they allow themselves together, the more tangled they become. The more steps they take between them, the more strangled and estranged.

This is the closest J's come to understanding. As it's as close as he's come to forgiving. But he's not ready yet to understand it fully. Because it's not only his to explain. Only his for that time to conjure. To work his magics upon his selves. Align his wills of man toward the only chance he sees. The mindless promise which has defined him for so long. The one he has to take the long way round to get to.

So it goes. So he remembers.

He remembers finding M fascinating. Months of unrelenting intrigue, and narcotic satisfaction, to be chosen by the one he chose. Two souls uniting in rainstorms and nighttimes as the only two creatures upon the blessed earth. It was them, despite the rest of them ever having been, warm through the coldest winter, right through the deepest wrong.

Until M, J had never known what it was like to be alone. He'd always been alone, he'd just never known there was another way. M's the first person J ever truly met. As though he'd never before crossed what distance exists between two people. M is J's first love. M was J's first lover. M's the only one J's ever seen fit to choose. This may be the only thing that J's never doubted.

It took an entire year for J to word it right, to court him properly, dropping notes on an impassable threshold into a world he could not know. Then, on the first new moon, on the 2nd of January, the year 2002, they spent their first night together, then never another apart. A clumsy newborn zealot holding his newfound ivory idol for the first night as he would for years of nights to come. Never one without the other, whether there or obviously not.

M taught J balance, M taught J grace, by leaping bravely from rock to rock along shorelines in the nighttime. J glowed brightly like a beacon, played the matron anchor, as M's worlds kept falling apart. M let J feel pride by being able to see what J'd never been able to show another. J let M feel safe by not being able to see any reason why not to love him.

Unimaginable things interrupted. Nobody died but people were killed. Hearts, to make them beat, were pounded.

"I will forgive you, when you ask me to. Will you forgive me too?"

It's time for his heart's endeavor to choose to which pride to adhere. So J's gone about making progress with what he's so long held restrained. His life's by no means alright. His days are not the same. He wants more than just memories. All these thoughts he can't forget. He's tried to wander backwards, off to the side, it's done only so much good. So back, with fervor, to a forward he can't surrender. To hasten one end, and to skirt one doom, to see what lies beyond.

J goes about buying a home on Bloor Street for them to grow in, racing impossibilities within his mind. Those parts that believe him rightly deserving and those saboteurs he needs to violently convince. Better destroy. He spends his days constructing a surer safety so that M might come home so that what's to come might finally begin. Well-journeyed potentials finally combined, unleashed then dared to be free.

He calls upon his greatest skill and makes the story true. Believing that there comes a time of payments due for all their prices paid. He reaches into the deepest pockets of what's possible amongst what maybe only he can see. Despite wills all around him, he corrals circumstance with effort, hope and belief. He prays to godforms as humbly as he can muster, beseeching outcomes from both sides.

There's no reason why they can't be happy.

It's time to forego what's kept them simple. They need each other. It's time to take cues from all the small analogies so obviously all around. They're the chosen ones who've held on for so long. Dragged skinless, refusing to let go of an overwhelming power that neither could control. A four-handled thing that they both tried to hold alone. It's time to recognize the wills with which they're dealing. Time to humbly be half of something greater as it implies being part of something more.

11. No home on Bloor. There's a distinction between writing about your life and living it. If you're a simple man, the distinction is clear. First comes the story, then comes its telling. The path lies plainly before you. You never doubt this or seek alternatives, if you're a simple man.

If you're a writer, it's a matter of time. You know what's most important isn't the story itself rather the memory of how it might've been told as a means to recount it more. In every culture, the clerics are the first people to write things down. They're the first to spell.

So there's no home on Bloor even though J wrote it down and everything he's ever written has come true. He must not have worded it well or there are obviously still other wills involved. In any case, the house on Bloor was being run as a boarding house. J intended to make it a home but the money-lenders and the money-keepers don't like the sort of clientele that such a place draws. With no way of policing how the house will be used, beyond the worth of a man's words, they prefer not to associate with that sort of people. Those people who need help. Those who are in trouble. Who have only their words to offer. But that's neither here nor there.

Apparently, J's lost the plot. Such a horrible thing when you're a writer. Always somewhere between the plot and the grave. Only noticing, in periphery, that the two might overlap. That a plot might be a grave, summarily, the place a person held in their life. Their lot. Marked by words someone else etched in stone. Which makes a plotline either the direction in which a story flows or the line which connects two formerly distinct things together. As "to plot it" is to walk the distance between two histories, whether by footstep or intent to will.

There's a beautiful word, *complot*. At present, for J, it exists as does a wishbone in the breast of some flying bird. He doesn't know how to use it. To reach it, he must learn to fly higher than he's so far been able to or to coo sweetly enough to call it near. Near enough to rip out its chestbone. If one happens to be so desperate for a chance to make a wish that they could kill a winged thing. Which he is not. Or one might simply have patience as that wish naturally matures. Never rushed enough to make foolish leaps. Always calm enough to practice calling. Maybe even someday wise enough to lay down seed. To finally deserve that chance, when the feathered thing's nest's surrendered, that chance at a happy ending, peacefully availed.

Besides, with a wishbone, it's only a fifty-fifty chance of one bone, of one's wish granting, unless both hands pulling are commonly intended. In which case, the bone need not even be torn, simply worn as a talisman. An instruction biologically unearthed. Like a tree trunk followed, branching as far as green when reaching skyward or down toward one and the solid earth. So, there's a wish to be made when a bird dies. Otherwise, the power of the charm is wasted, charged all its life near the heart aflight of a bird in the skies who's wandered.

So J returns to his writing. He believes that he's the best at something because he loves it so. He returns to it to help him understand. Because he loved that home, like he loves that man, and he can't understand why both have, over time, destructed. He now sees that his writing is his soothing future. It's the place, by the lake, where he built a fort as a child. The stones of which are still there, as he'd ordered them, whenever he visits.

Revisits markers he's dropped along the way, trying to reorient, figure out how he's strayed in his search for answers and outcomes, preferring some, deferring others, erasing mistaken ones by walking back. Trying on lives and estimating futures. Noting the ways in which he's tried and the ways he might still muster to somehow accommodate the boy in the neighborhood who he's not supposed to play with anymore because he's nothing but trouble and no good'll ever come of him.

But M doesn't have any other brothers than him. And J kinda feels sorry. Kinda feels the same. As does everybody else, probably, he guesses.

Despite the ways, which mark the days, in which J's not like any other. The things he can do, the things he is doing and the crazy things he'll someday dare. You probably can't even tell. But it's true. He's brave, in these moments, when his fleshy insides are half as relevant as the shiny things his hands are shaping. Cleverly distracted, having swapped a will to affect for his cruelly innate will to be affected. Just to get it out of him, into plain sight, to see it and call it saboteur.

The only lesson he's fully learned, in twenty thousand words of his manuscript, is that his scrutiny has the so-far unrestrainable power to abolish. Seems, for him to find it fascinating is for him to wish it away. Is for him to misguidedly direct his powerful will to the premature naming of something he wants to get to know. Which certainly implies that sewn into his lover's caress is a grip at another's reality and a subtler sense of something stirring. Provided his word can be trusted when it explains what his words truly say. This is him searching for truth in his nature so that he can stare it in the face and rest his eyes, for a time, from the furious sun. So he does. He tries to turn his power against himself so he can stop playing little boys' games.

M's been calling, for months, for J's attention, leaving the numbers where he can be reached, begging for him to call back. But J never does. He never knows which M is calling or from whose shelter or how and too many memories trigger avalanches. He's mapped every trap by tripping them and won't waste any time reliving what's futile, down paths that have led to dead ends. J holds onto only one memory and waits for M to approach him recognizably. Until then, he has no reason to call a stranger's house. It doesn't matter that J can reach him if M can still run away. He who has hunted, he who is hunted, soon tires, soon learns to set traps.

Twenty thousand words, so far, trying to construct what M could've just whispered in his ear. There's no use lamenting something that's passed. Possibility travels forward into time, impossibility back. Now, even asking for it is reaching too far. He's not moving any further for M's explanations. Not even so little as asking. There's only one way to make a body forget what a mind has found better ways to remember. You have to make it feel something stronger or more convincing. Especially when dealing with feelings that resound, knowing echoes in a tinman quickly deafen.

He's never physically forgotten what it's like to be betrayed. He wears it still in the lining of his chest. Where, with M, he could simply pour it away. Where, without him, the pressure keeps redoubling.

Regardless, M's not here and there's a life to be lived. The one that J killed himself to get to and will kill again, if he has to, whatever gets in his way. Let me spell it out for you. Any surplus of energy is something J thinks he can use. And he's coursing with it. All the things he's swallowed have caused chains of implosions. He's found a way of accessing possibility like never before and he's trying clumsily to teach himself the will to manifest by recognizing the wills of his saboteurs. The whole world changes when a man dreams something possible and himself capable of it. It usually becomes a crisper green.

Understand, J *has* to build a home. Just like he *has* to get him back. These are his single will of man despite the parts of himself that he can't rely on. There's no other future he's able to conceive of, or to work toward, or to convince himself worth living. Not yet anyway. So he dares every footstep fearing that he might still fail. Afraid to mistakenly take the one step that might matter with the wrong foot. Still, he hacks blindly away at inevitability, convinced that his will exists whether or not it can affect the unfolding of any man's path. He spends his time swapping futilities, one that would sacrifice a life for one that would take a chance at two. It's the consequenceless barter he dares to make despite his fallible awareness of time.

The man who fails at everything he tries should try his hand at failing. J's chosen to devote his time to an exploration of paradoxes of perspective. He's chosen fascination as the expression of his sincerest flatteries, knowing full well that the glare of his awe obliterates. If he was a duller man, or one smaller, he might find some continuity or something lasting to his devotions. As it stands, he's too clever a man to find anything fascinating for very long. He too soon understands the things he finds beguiling, enough to say their names and explain away their guile. Except for M, who seems to have doomed J to impossibility. Who left J trying to disbelieve the facts he must consider by changing the order in which they fall. With what he knows, J fails should he understand him and he fails should he fail to.

The stakes are too high and, for the first time, J sees that M was right to have stepped away.

"He defines me."

Thoughts of that M and that life are woven into every effort J makes. From the home he intends to build, to the razor-wire filter he's about to put between them, to the direction his life is pointed. He sits ailing over every one of these words, trying to explain it perfectly. To prepare a place for reconciliation at the end of a long hallway decorated with stations depicting the worst of it.

M never says a word. Regardless, they've been revealed. J's been exposed as an ailing spirit. Though he'll try to convince you that he's just convalescing. M, as his opposite, is thereby exactly the same. It's hunched them. You can see that their chests are tight and their backs hurt.

Don't underestimate how determined J is to make these things happen. The will is cellular. He will find a home and he will live in it with M. Just as he pulled all the rest of it down on top of him. Even if he has to wrestle with the most powerful parts of himself or anyone else. Even if he'll have to exhaust himself to do it. And he's already ailing. Though he's not really ailing, now, is he? The disease he has is incurable.

Whatever salvation he might've hoped to uncover by shouting that particular demon's name only serves to reveal a more terrifying parallel: The face and the eyes in every shadow. Any writer knows that if something is true on one level then it must be true on every level. It's the only way man might know god or the true sense of himself in his own life forced into reality by the perfect pronunciation. He can never forget that his life bears a hard edge despite the lightness of the things he's thinking.

There's a line where the two dimensions of words on a page extend into three in the real world. Upon it sits the matrix that must be used to translate between the two. Somewhere between a man's brain and his experience of having it. As a soul is just the incomplete manifestation of man, always leaving something like a shadow underneath all of his creations. It's the nature of tactility itself that darkness must be created when matter exists to block the light. J notes this as he trods along, explaining away the impurities he keeps finding in his person.

So it must be, by the end of it, that M's a bad person, in deed if not intention, whether by choice or another will, as M's told J all along although J could never hear it. Regardless, by now J's been through every conceivable excuse and none coincide with the facts of M's character. So it must be. He's the wicked result of a little boy's choice to let himself be hurt because he wanted to see what that feels like. Or worse, because it turned him on. It's in his choices, his reactions and the way the rubble falls when his worlds fall apart. So J's forced to realize that he's in the purest love with a bad man and what that says about him.

There's no denying it. He's seen himself reduced to his subleast. He hears himself plotting metaphors about the depth of M's depravity raising his own immodest morality to higher heights. For the rest of his life, he'll bear their disgrace as proof of it. Still, he should've known better than to grab a horned thing's tail to keep it from falling. Never believe you're helping when you grab the tail of a horned thing to keep it from falling. Especially if you're enamored with it. It wants to get back down into the pits from whence it came. No. What you should do is let it escape, take with it what it can't help but know from its time in your world and watch the infection spread.

So, it seems, all along it was a duel. J must've let M choose the weapon. He must not have been thinking. So excited for the chance at a lasting spar with a worthy partner that he brushed over what should've been fear. Overlooked the fact that every choice we make traps us in paradigm. J woke to suddenly find himself fighting when what he was really trying to do was follow rabbits.

Regardless, following rabbits, chasing demons, it doesn't matter when you suddenly find yourself in holy war. It only matters that certain blows, against certain foes, demand that a player leave himself vitally exposed in order to strike them, should it be necessary to strike them. In this moment a man must weigh, most clearly, choice and consequence. It's never enough time.

Before this, J was Bodhisattva, a harbinger, to each, of his own. Now he has a demon following him, demanding all of his attention, or a small legion. He must turn his fascination on them. They're the tiny saboteurs he's used to excuse his fault in his grossest horrors. Witness to his own errors of divinity. They've embedded him in a progressionless future where he's forced to grow fractally, making more intricate an already complex thing. Like cancer would.

J's allowed himself a broader range of possibility by simultaneously realizing polar truths. At first, it only served to confound insomuch as his wills conflicted. Later, it revealed which had the strongest power to exert.

On the subtlest level of his consciousness, J remembers restraining possibilities. Although time obscures the image, he sees his own hand forcing his path to veer from craving to compulsion but he can't see why. Nor can he yet see the purpose.

J sees only all the promises he lost to the tsunami of what he'd then have to endure. Of what an arrogant will might manifest. Like that time the guy he loved got viruses in his cum then got cum in his eye and he knew that the rest of his forever wasn't going to be the same. This is the truth of it that must be noted: He got cum in his eye. This truth must be made clear enough to replace choice and chance in the mind of anyone who might stumble on it. He doesn't know how to use this truth quite yet. He just feels it impending. It can't be explained any more clearly than that, not by such a young man, that there's a sense of inevitability underneath all the other things going on.

12. This is faery tale. This is the telling of a creature into life. One J's had to carve out of him. One he's not yet done sculpting. He awoke, lost on a bad path, already searching to find a truth that rips a hole in the story and lets him peer through. He's come face to face with his destroyer and he's now demanding, from it, cues to life.

He risked a life, one he had no right to risk, because it seemed worth it and he lost. Awed by the stakes of the wager. Blinded, by possibilities, to likelihoods. This doesn't make him a fool. It makes him foolhardy. And a loser, only because he lost. So the game's over and, in some sense, he's won. Won rights to a deathless place he sought in contrasts.

Somedays, the clicking of things falling into place sounds like a hailstorm on a tin roof. Somedays, J gets lost to it and exists only as discrepancies in the patterns of his mechanisms of character. Somedays, the most basic will to go on is the most he can muster. He gets claustrophobic in the things he needs from the world to the point where every action becomes a panic reflex. He gets primitive with it and prone to mortal errors. He's been charged with his graces. He's been made too aware of his meats.

Man is the incomplete manifestation of the soul. Somewhere between animal and pure light. Should it manifest itself more completely and man would be a simpler creature but he'd have no soul. Any less and he wouldn't matter at all.

"What's the matter, Honey?"

In both directions, J's lost years of his life. Enough to know that the price of some days will age you months. And that the consequences of willlessness are as plainly horrific as any you might suffer by willing. Of this he's sure, that will has nothing to do with choice and thereby consequence. Which doesn't explain why he still blames M for the way things are between them now. Why he holds M accountable for every time he could not or can't. Otherwise, the face that J cannot reach through is something solid and impenetrable, earthbound, and he should move on.

The earthbound should be pitied, and their nature revered, for their sacrifice of soul offers the skyward a sense of direction. They're the monsters of lore of failed ascendings. Broken mirrors that must remain as anchors to keep the tether taut for the sure man. The only man who's certain that his path climbs up to heaven with him so positive of his swiftness and his path as to wear an adamantine tether around his neck to let them know the way. To begin the new descending. They'll pull heaven down on top of them by the weight of what they've done.

Just as M and J have a cycling way of leaving one to tend to the meats while the other goes off soaring meatless. Though they're never really apart. Sewn microscopically together by an adamantine thread, threaded through the eye.

Never really sure which end is which, J searches himself for signs of the arrival of the time to do remarkable things. Or for some signs of parting. His senses hasten when he thinks about wandering. About wandering into the great oblivion and trying, through contrast, to take back his life from the hands of his tumbleweed gods. Searching along the extents of himself to be able to scream, "I did it. I fucking did it." To erase any notion that maybe he shouldn't have. To nullify the concept that maybe he couldn't. But time doesn't travel in that direction and he has no more life to spare for a moment that's changed. So the searching stops but not the wander and the genesis is set to begin.

That's the progression of that. Explained by forms solidifying on roadsides. J brought M back. He told you he would. He got them a house on Fairview. He told you he would. J's using all the words to say this just right. Even though he's sure it'll take only three. And he spent the first night in their new home together too afraid to fall asleep. With that look in M's yellow eyes, muttering something about how J changed the color of his hair and raped him. So much like those days when he used to accuse J of drugging him and stealing his sperm to impregnate his friends.

Just another in a line of commonplace lunacies that J chose the opposite of away from.

So he blinks, not to see, when he has to.

J's always been drawn choicelessly to M. Or thereabouts. As truly as simply wanting pain will bring it to you. Even a childish curiosity can trap you in moments you haven't chosen. M traps J in moments he hasn't chosen. Knowing full well that it's easier to suffer than it is to not suffer but unable to affect a thing. Leaving him here, loyal to a disloyal man. Wherever he is and whoever's there with him. Unclear about why he's enduring but trying to figure out the person he's creating. While, aside, the things he does happen. Unfold like a story, like a ball rolling down a hill, as his guide to how it all ends up settling. Depending upon the mistakes he's made and how neatly he's hidden them away with all the other things he finds he now has to hide in order to amass life. Faced with all the things he should've done, and all the things he shouldn't have, pouring down like blessings into the stories he tells, like the northern lights come down to see, sparkling insights, along the way, as he searches for a cure. Some way to end his trance and transcend.

Once he was justly righteous. If you overlook the ego it takes to deem something brilliant. Once, in an infinite instant, is more than enough. It's an eternity for any thought to be replaced by any other or for any wandering sensation to be smeared across the spectrum into white light until there seems only one certainty to life beyond all contradicting truths within. Which J believes lays somewhere between the importance of loving M and his inability to explain it properly.

It used to be that J would always run home to M. Or thereabouts. What surrounds M is J's obsession. What he can make of it. Keys to doors to places he's never fast enough to pass through. Changing form as quickly as his eyes are able to perceive them. Revealing who he is by what he recognizes, knowing full well that identity's autocannibalistic and that all things autocannibalistic are trapped in Midgaard's kiss. They must learn to grow more quickly than they devour like J's compulsion to continue to try. To try to interpret his feelings with the higher functions of his mind. Even though one is voluntary and one is not. And one's will's best kept from affecting the other.

Now, J stands behind M. Only so the line that connects him to his fate passes directly through M's chest as well. So that what connects them does so like lightning does the earth and sky. J's right in that regard, insofar as holding faith that their heavy horrors might be anchor to such a light lightness. Act as footweight, holding ground for them in the playtime for the gods he would bring.

J's held both halves of it. Just at different times. So he knows it's possible.

But that's not quite how the story goes, depending on whether you're looking at the cycle or noting the spiral. Either way, in this story soon, the hand of god will intervene and everything will change. Which rarely makes for good storytelling unless, in some clever way, the name of god is uttered when he enters. Which, to a man of words, is all different kinds of fun.

So, J called M back and M came back. That first night, one month before J built a home around them, M came back to J and they fucked themselves to sleep. They sweated and grunted and dirty fucked all night through. Through imagined memories of times gone by to herald ideas of new days descending. By the end of it, exhausted, they lay crossed at the legs, like babyfrogs, ass to ass. Siamese spirits connected at the core, ascending oppositeways through the bodies of two hurt boys. But what was rekindled was not love, not right away, not that night, not for the sake of the act of loving or for the reenactment of having once loved. It was the blissful reliving of those first three months they spent together where a boy, born all knotted up, was untied and shown his tendrils.

The first day of a new hope is the only day it shines its brightest.

Then things went wrong with them. As they always do. And on and on. This time round, tumbling all the more rapid, polishing one and leaving the other to dull, over months of silly taunting. Strobes of a chance at a brilliant future in between grey solid slabs of unmoving earthen monotones.

Doctors called M's name, called him schizophrenic, at J's request. He was summarily proclaimed guilty and absolved of all responsibility. The slate was, for a moment, clean. Numbers were given. Appointments made. Potions administered. It was a hopeful time. The yellow disappeared from M's eyes but he suddenly got too fat. So sleepy, with potion, and hungry too. He ate all the bananas in the banana hole, was too fat to get out and had to die there. So he died there in a slump of unachieved self. He had his lover, his home, his mind, his safety, his life, everything he needed to go on but he couldn't. Couldn't make it work. Couldn't see the puzzle with all its pieces whole. Couldn't stop seeing cracks where the cracks had been glued together. Not after what he'd done. That's not how his eyes were able to make sense of things. The weight of what J thought he'd dispelled was more powerful a presence to M than the hand on the body of the man who'd pulled him free because the way that he pulled him free was his own condemnation and that seemed too steep a price to pay to a boy who woke to find himself worthless.

Instead of warm grace and tact and a genuine thankful embrace, M pulled away from J. With shame and guilt, he had to hide his face for having killed him. Or so he said. M couldn't reach back, couldn't mistake J's hold for anything but choking, which J couldn't accept or understand, nor could he plead anymore loudly for a hand now that he could finally see that he needed it. So a fissure formed in the quaking earth. Everything, once worth fighting for, tore and opened up as distance between them.

"I loved you. All the way through when it happened to me. I guess you think it's different for you somehow."

J gave to M a perfectly worded world. The name of self. All his explanations, all the instructions needed to advance him immeasurably, accelerate him indefinitely. Turns out, for at least too long as to be not soon enough, M was just a little boy underneath it all, cowering from boogeymen. Not capable of the things J would force from him. Too cold and afraid of what he now knew he'd imagined. That he couldn't take a single step into the real world where there were real people doing real things. Not for the sake of what he'd forsaken, nor for the sake of what another man had. It wasn't easy anymore in a world where there was fault and M had only ever done what was easiest. Less even, if some other force could be laid back into.

J'd taken the turtle shell that M was using as a mask and called for him to come out. Little naked turtle boy. M just laughed at him. Laughed at J for even trying, knowing all the while that there can be no love from a shellless naked turtle boy.

It was no longer easy and M was afraid. Convinced that he was useless and withered and wasted. M was terrified and tried to keep them somehow together by holding on so tightly to whatever he was holding because he believed he couldn't do it alone. Arms crossed over a muffled regardless thing so tightly that J grew jealous to see it. To look at what he couldn't know would drive them apart to see. Wasting J's time.

Until, finally, exhausted by more than one struggle, M had to let go. It was a ridiculous tug of war between a desperate schizophrenic streetkid and a supergenius seeking archnemeses. Over the rotting remains of an unrealized potential that was never more than an aspect of J's delirium. His lovesickness. Which just goes to show the true nature of M's regard for J. That he would trick him, take love from him with lies and grabbing and hiding. Treat him like any of the other men he'd fucked for a place to stay.

So it seems every man's reality is some version of insane. For some people it takes the form of hysteria and they go around simply laughing. Some people take off all of their clothes and run around in the snow. Some give away their money on street corners and talk to woodsprites and fairygnomes. M took his truths to godawful places and dragged the best parts of the good people around him down into the dirty depths to be devoured along with him.

M knew they were coming for him and that it was only a matter of time before they arrived. He chose to submit to this. J watched him make the same decision every time he had to choose. This was the truth of what J cared for. That M had given up. Anymore, he was only echoes in a tinman resounding. A thousand times, M could be sanctioned or explained, understood or cured, but there would always be something. With M, there was always going to be something.

Something had ripped and M was holding it together with no hand free to reach for anything else. J was a fool to have expected different. At least not so quickly. After seeing what he'd done to get to him, J found that he couldn't wait. He'd done all that he could do, given all that he had, and his role in this man's fate was satisfied. He got M help. He went where M had wandered and he did what it took to bring him back. So they could stand face to face and make the choice. J could do no more for whatever answer he expected of happily ever after. Not even wait for it. He'd spared all the life he could. He knew true terror at the true sight of his real lover in the raw.

So they're not together. J needs for there to be love and M's clearly incapable of it. Unable to let go. He's terrified to fall into the sun like all things that thrive on rot. J's instinct is to crave wholeness and M was made broken. He's supposed to be that way. By his own inability to will. M was shards of a man that J spent his time arranging because he just had to look into the green eyes of the picture of his perfect lover to see if the cracks might fuse. J did all he could do to put him back together. His lover got sick and he took care of him but M's kinds of diseases can't be cured. He was cracked. J's lover never was to ever love him anymore. Which is a series of paradoxes that J counters with logic. With: What has a beginning must have an end. Which is every excuse he needs to spiral off. To go searching for something more eternal that he's been searching for all along, just in the wrong places. So goodbye.

J uses his instinct to crave, on levels he still hasn't imagined, to somehow summon, down from heaven, the hand of god.

13. The hand of God. A man need only be convinced of the possibility of his own greatness for a chain of events to begin to amplify. It's that moment, however, before disbelief can be suspended, that holds men most their days. The slightest notion that maybe he can't. Or the involvement of some will outside his own. Some brilliant exemplar who he fears he mightn't follow or the sight of someone obviously confined to make him suspect. The nature that is the conundrum of man.

Both ways in time, infinities of cause and consequence expand conically from the moment they explain. A pin-point now has gathered bothways from possibility to shimmer as one man's hour. He has ancestry to anticipate him and legacy to enshrine. Though none of it matters because none of it's any more real than his latest fickle version of it. There's really only one man, despite how fractured, or however the details arranged, and there's really only one moment of which he's ever been aware.

He's born human and raised to be a man. Just as every chicken hatches from an egg even though chickens are not the only creatures to lay them. Man is born soft. He's all sense and wonder. Born to named creatures who need not be named here. If you know a creature's name then you can take away its power. It takes only the perfect pronunciation. Provided the context is of any relevance at all.

Only an arrogant fool believes that this moment is about him. One so absorbed of self that he could absently take the life of another. When a child is born, it's the mother who bleeds, as the world goes through her to get him. To drag him, to tag him, to cut the tie that binds him to what might hint at something whole. To keep him from explaining what will only confound by quickly teaching him to want, by calling him a name and telling him that he's lacking. Forcing into him a sense of something missing, something coming for which he must begin to search, implied bothways in time. Whereto and wherefrom.

When he's torn from a nameless place into a world of clans, first he's dreamed of, then given half his own name, half a name that's someone else's. A once endless thing is then as best defined, confined within the extents of what an already limited other might be able to conceive. So begins the spell he must work his way from under.

Words, when spoken, which begin to set his skin and fuse his bones. Merge his identity around him to confine the light inside. This is his curse. Subjectivity becomes the conundrum of man. The clever trap of perspective nurtured fast around him. Though it's done in earnest loving that he's taken from simple experience and given title so that he might explain what he'll soon forget of what he can never understand for the sake of how pretty his face is. It's just the cycle tumbling as frightened aging beings try to protect. That named ones give names to the otherwise perfectly purposed and a formerly soft thing becomes hard and heavy.

Until a child's skull fuses, his brain exists in a narcotic state of absorptive ecstasy. His experience of self is the experience of existing until the word "eye" becomes the notion "I" and all insight changes. He becomes a man, amongst men, and is taught to crave a lesser purpose. Distracted down to five senses and the woes that stem from the insufficient sense he can make of them. Feelings are taken from fingertips and made halftales of demiurges. What was once a soothing silence becomes a cacophony of thoughts. Some he remembers, others he thinks.

A fire cannot be understood by looking at the flames. The fire's just what becomes of whatever it is that's burning. Becoming man is exactly that, only the other way in time. The gathering of all the light it takes to make a diamond. The inevitability, within some infinity, that patterns will emerge. And a man wakes on the surface of himself, holding down his self, scrambling to make sense of what was sense all along before the construct of him got involved and couldn't begin to understand.

Consider a spiral, coiled into a spiral, coiled into a spiral itself. And on and on in both directions. Any pattern made of patterns unending. Take it only so far as the dawning of some sense of something familiar and trust that no man's mind can know it any further. Take a moment's heed of this new sense of yours, tingling, then consider what it would mean to travel this path. Conceptually, say a beam of light. Some path that takes the speed and the dimension of something infinite and connects it fractally to its oblivious counterpart. So that, at some point, something, that might be nothing more than the pattern itself, might become so involved in tracing its way heavenward, or otherwise, that some creature, situated just right in space and time, might take that nothing, all knotted up, and hold it in its hand.

It's in this way that man's connected to god and that god's connected, through man, to nothing at all. Or to what exists, beyond material's concern, of the immaterial's will to be. The weave of conflicting forevers, out of the deep dark directionless down, into the idea of man.

Man stands as an eventuality when all the light it takes to make a diamond decides that it might be bound. Such is the conundrum of man. That all he comprises must be bound into his being. And thereby, that all he comprises must be bound in it as well. He stands as the gateway, keeper of his own prison, too capable of concept to be trusted with the unraveling of all the light it takes to undo what has been done for the sake of the chance at being.

When existence became a possibility, all those things that did not exist jumped at the chance. Man's begun to remember this and it can paralyze. Whether relevant, or real, or valid, or otherwise. For the chance to be, he must be made amnesiac. Only to spend his days trying to climb higher than his self in order to see through the haze. Any chance to glimpse the true colour, which his subtlest nature insistently suspects, of the nighttime. Climb away from the earth's hold, opposite the water's flow, to where the thin air cannot be gathered into breathfuls, reaching for the place where the sun's fire becomes the northern lights. To remember a time when he was lighter. To satisfy his nagging suspicion that he might actually have a soul.

It can be said no more clearly than that. Now is man's most pivotal moment. More and more often he catches a sense of the veil thinning. As man's circumstance aligns and coincides just enough to sense patterns in the sun's light flashing off of wave tips. If he should he dare believe. Knowing, that the less a man believes of the raging things inside, the greater the swing of his pendulum rides. Especially in times when his broken parts let through cracks of light and he can't help but begin to dazzle. Charm himself from the inside out, caught in the mirror's sway. When he's forced to allow for the wandering of his meats in order to see the equation of infinities balance. By coming near enough to his own willful annihilation to calculate how much must be sacrificed for how much gained and what he might call into reality by sacrificing his tail for a teaspoon of light.

Suddenly, J caught sight of his own reflection, maybe in M's glazed-over eyes, and he knew true panic when he couldn't name the thing that he'd become. Thereby earthbound by the power it held over him. Nor could J ask the traitor zombie that was left of the man he'd once risked everything to love. Only two devils left and everywhere hell. Which is absolute, if forced to commit to it, and proof enough, suddenly, of god.

So the hand of god, summoned from heaven descends, and J's cured. It makes no sense and nobody's going to believe it. Even though nobody's the only man who can be trusted. Mr. NoBody and all his beans, whose path is no more bound by tendency, having considered the implication of what might happen should will and an awareness of inclination coincide. Like the chance that a light might shine so bright that all the world be disinfected. Leaving none a threat to any other and any one no threat to none. So it happened by contrast. By the accidental will of a man stripped of all his futures. That he willed the implosion of his moment and destroyed everything that he knew.

To wake in hell is to be convinced of heaven.

This, so far, has been a tragedy. The names of demons have been written and other things that gnaw. All there is to learn here, really, is that there are people trapped in this world who have the power to make you feel horrible things. If you don't want to feel these things you must never fall into this trap by finding any reason to love any one of these people at all. Turn your face away and go about a simpler life. If it's the extents of what your form and your intellect are capable of bearing, or generating, that you wish to explore then you must do the precise opposite. You must find any way to know how to love any one of them at all. Risk whatever price, whatever cost or cage, for a running start to remember your brilliance beyond it. To express and finally be able to see the absolute consuming rapturous truth that you've only ever been a pattern of light. By extremes, you must rip a chasm between the expressions of yourselves. Wide enough that the mediocre null space in between you feels like falling, falling out of reason for being, should any aspect of your awareness laze.

No story has a happy ending. The violent experiencing of now is the essence of every story ever told. Pulled, by some awareness, from the bright white light. Every aspect of this moment is about the maintaining of the firmament, about the curious notion that consequence is the price of being. And that being must, by its nature, resist any will toward complacent life or any sort of nonfurthering. Let alone an end. If it has a beginning then it must have an end. It can be coiled up into a spiral. It exists as a singularity amidst what's its opposite and eternal. They define one another. Torment and rhapsody have a common border. They are opposite and thereby equal.

Eternity is everything, is nothing, is the uniform instantaneous alltime, boring enough for ethereal nonbeings to crave and settle for meatsuits for the simple sake of consequence. Even if it turns out that will's not enough to sustain. It was worth it to see the true magic of a pinpoint moment's order within a chaotic nonoblivion. To wield the contrast of two netherregions like a wrecking ball, one dimensionless and one omnidimensioned, to hint at what god might worship.

The simplest beauty is a thing found possible. Within or without you, across realities and all that's not real. J had to learn this the hardest way. That the greatest gift is time, to one whose time is measured, or to one who's got no time at all. So's the greatest theft, incurring the stiffest penalties. Summarily, and without further hesitation, thereby M be banished.

If you must defend against it then it's your enemy. If you have any enemy at all then you've failed and have committed yourself to irrelevance. The story is not for you, it's about you, and will drag you along because you wrongly care. Either way, you must submit and be absorbed by it. To the evilest vile should your most brilliant brilliance be less easily achieved. Or should it somehow unwind. You must tend toward whatever oneness you're capable. This is the only way to see reason beyond the things men do. To understand for what you're being prepared.

Halfway through a tale told, at J's most desperate moment, the contrast of absolutes forces his hand. He reaches, holding ashes of a brilliance denied for the sake of some misery's purest, most selfful obscurity. One violently thrust upon him by the steepest failing of the only nameless man whose name he'd ever tried to speak.

In his last, saddest effort, J sends two letters, sending ripples bothways in time. One backward, bounced off the past, in which he asks M to come back to him. One forward, into the future, to a time now made paradox. Unconsciously wagering that someway the name of god might be the only sound audible after all prayer has failed and every other truth has faded. It's his only hope that the one word uttered at the beginning of creation might echo somehow in the harmony of his unchanging heart's beseeching for any idea how to be realized.

But time travels only in one direction and the letter J sends into the future arrives first. Before M might scratch away the last thread dangling. It summons a boy named L from a past that hasn't happened yet. His arrival is much like the smiting away, by the hand of god, of the failure of a lifetime's devotion. To a cycling moment that could never know a good man's deserved fruition because of the bad path he followed to get there.

Playing naughty games in the treehouse with his brother, M and his infectious taste for taboos. The same way, L reminds J of his hot cousin and that just turns him on. Into him, he sees him morph, sometimes when they kiss. In a glimmer, in an eye. With a hand on a hip, naked in the starlight, steaming in the snow. In a laugh and a confusion of histories, travelling wrongways through time, overlapping all the details. Somehow equating the unlikelihood that they've met with the impossibility that they've known each other all along. For the sake of a divinely granted reprieve from their paths for no reason they care to know.

Armed guards stand, with their backs to a locked door, while two familiar strangers orbit. Their days together have this sense of reverse captivity. Of being caged in a world that's not free. Before both must, back to it, return unbound.

They spend a week together in which J goes supernova. Into the fiery sun, he ascends and stands unblinded. Engulfed in the white sunlight in which he's been trying to bask with M for years. Believing and accepting that he must be drugged, and caged, and beaten, and bound, in order to transcend. From a world where he measures the distances between things to one where he just assumes. Though it's different with L. It's a freeman's choice and, as consequenceless freemen, they make days of perfect love. So perfect and flawless that J should've known it wouldn't be allowed to last.

J's the first to sense this chance between them. He steps into L to kiss, to slide a lover's hand underneath to find L's unflawed flesh, so tight, so smooth. Warm against a nubile man, who's seen his face and called his name, is all J's reason to writhe. To explore. To slide into the nude air himself. His cock hard and ready since L first saw him inside. When he said that thing that he said that never mattered. That brought him to him. So his hands could reach, when he had a right to hold, to search for tactile truths. When he could finally make the full claim of brethren and be fully fucked over. J doesn't hesitate to lean in. To suck and slither, suddenly interested only in siphoning the flow when, beyond it all, they're finally together.

Two new moons round the world in orbits. In swells, tides gather, raise round two moonboy avatars. So they kiss, in the crashing waves, and fall into the sand. Where the earth tries to swallow them and the water wash away. L's huge cock is enough to tear the layer in between them. It bounds into the air and J takes hold of it. It tastes like seasalt. There's no time here, so no words are spoken. Not after the spell's been cast. J pulls him in as soon as he can. They, as brothers, flip flop fuck, in the sunlight become moonlight, while their moons trade eclipsing suns. Across each others' borders, they fuck atomically through the lines meant to keep them apart.

They bleed light into the other with every caress, every taste across unnoticed inbetweens. One and the other and what's up and what's down. Blood, from insides, becomes sweat, and comes out, and cum, and's swallowed, becomes blood, and comes out, and salts, becomes sticky between them. Kisses fold realities hold and serpents in caverns swell. The sound of the circuitous flow is deafening.

L's cocktip glistens with his frenzy. Drips his fervor against puckering holes to ease the pain when what must rip, does, to let two things no longer apart. His animal pumps and swoons, slides gently in. He must either be a fool or a wiseman. No matter, he slides fearlessly in, turgid next a covetous ass. J drinks dry their moist tongues tied as Midgaard grows, as the world slows. Though the hunger, in this moment, is sated. J's shown why. Why he's never quitted. With a tongue in his mouth and a cock in his ass, why his death was less a doorway barred, never threatening enough to keep his head from banging. He finds a key and another door, both of which L holds claim to, waves his hand and lets J know.

On the third day, J gives L a key to the home he built for M on Fairview. On the fourth day, J sees a glowing portal through which he might pass. On the fifth day, each tells the other that he loves him when they part, when J delivers L back to his way and goes about his own.

This psychotic episode lasts one full week. One full week before the L worth loving is replaced by cultish Armaggedonists. Before he dies three times, finds Jesus and is brainwashed away. Nevermind. This just goes to prove that it was J's light. All along, it was all of what J's capable and no more.

It's a psychotic episode. This cannot be overlooked nor how truly terrifying. How eager J is to submit to the glow of a world begun to yellow. He loses himself to what he sees as the eyes of otherworldly godmen in five-dimensional patterns in treetops. Whispers withinbetween the sounds of radios overlapping with car parts humming and the squawking of seagulls wrestling over french fries.

Only when L's path no longer coincides with his own, does J gain clarity enough to see that he's forgotten about M and for what. Peace he found in the din resounding as hollow memory in the emptiness of his cold alone. Something he notes as it comes back to him. The world rebecomes a grey place when his lightness fades. When L goes away. When J's pulses slow and he can't gather breath enough to scream. No.

More and more the weight of it presses down. He fights to resist his heart's urge to lament. As he tries to unforget the taunting feeling that he's known things, that are gone now, that were brilliant. For a long while, he's frightened of this pull toward what he now sees as insane. But there's nothing else that makes sense to him. Only when there's nothing left again does he see it.

To echo with the sense of having seen this purest glow is to know that it's the only worthwhile thing that is. No meat, no mind, no curse of time can erase the sense of having sensed it. The bridge between what is this pinpoint oblivion and what is decidedly not. All possibility manifest.

J thinks he might've caught sight of a soul, through the doorway, out of the corner of his eye. And he's nearly willing to risk it all again, all that he's rebuilt and all that he's built on top of it, knowing that something that might pass for a soul has, at some point, been within eyesight.

J commits to finding his way back to that glowing portal through which he didn't take the chance to pass. Through which he's never been able to cross for the sake of the obvious truth that the way to salvation cannot be through another man without the other man being in the way. He sees now that he must do it alone. For the love he sought was an unconscious attempt at undoing, sewn into the basest nature of his being, in a universe where one plus one equals naught and boys who love boys are told not to.

A gifted man, according to his libran understanding, must carry and bear the awareness of such a curse. His experience of this reality demands it. He cannot contain the entirety of his truth so he must be capable of the force it would take to hold back something intent upon his annihilation. He might choose to remain a weak man and hope to draw no notice or he might be curious to see how the threat of his absolute genius might make his day a good one, bring to him love, and on into the night.

He vows to word it just right so that no M, no L, no named man might restrain it. So he won't be frightened when he reearns the chance, and the chance comes again, to summon it. When it's finally time to step that one foot through, knowing now that the proper combination of words, said to or by a receptive man, can reveal of him a Rockgodstar.

14. Light footsteps on the sun. When J says *writer* he thinks to himself *spellcaster*. As time degrades and things progress, he thinks he's found his creed. He's of the lineage Bodhisattva. He's Pilgrim Bodhisattva Harbinger Genii. Spellcaster. It's his place to say the word. He knows that the power of a spell's casting is not in how it's spoken or written, or woven, or done, it's in the way that it's received. Upon the same level upon which a man thinks his dreams are real.

A dream is the memory of some combination of experiences. J has recurring dreams of things he's only ever dreamed before, revealing something Midgaard about the way he likes to fall.

Resigned, it seems, to nighttimes, he remembers all the times the sun's burned blue's streaks into his eyes. With the road underfoot and the flies, in swarms, just buzzing. A pack on his back and every direction worth choosing. Simple prayers are prayed in daytimes, dragged into men's dreams by the setting sun. Making some men brave, and brave men defiant, enough to call into their dreams to challenge the universe for signs. Signs they must then follow. Which J did not. For which, he suffered a ten year curse and the price of at least one lifetime.

Dreams are an imprint in the medium of your awareness of what your mechanism might do. They're the weakest bridge between the physical and the metaphysical, all rickety, with planks missing. Like anything that goes sensed without consequence. Implying that now can only be the time it takes for us to process our experience, then to remember it.

So there's time between a man and what he knows. A moment, as fast as the time it takes the light to get to him, plus the time it takes for the light to get through.

A man has tools that he uses all his life to make order of what he sees. For a man to make sense sees us help god understand. Or god help us if we don't. Either way, man's left to his own devices. Left alone to conclude a coherent reality by his effort of experience. Capable of conclusions no more absurd than some idea of specks of light, a million miles apart, bound by unseen forces, into the lives of men. For each man, just a different kind of calculation and a different kind of proof.

The path of experience begins with reason for confusion, which leads to consideration, then a question spurs exploration, grabbing for some conclusion, until finally comes some form of acceptance of what a man might know. In this way, a man's confusion gathers order from his experience until the changing of some aspect of what's real causes him confusion again. And over and over. In the same way, science proved itself religion. Just as the fool sits next the genius on the spiral, only the long way round. One growing like a tree, the other like a cancer. Askew in their efforts and outcomes just enough to merit pride, which is a sin, as is identity, which is of dreams.

These are the things that J's will's learned trapped inside a slab of meat. To see a man confined is to see how to set him free. As other people's fascination will point a man, like a compass needle, to his own greatness. To that intentionless place where he shines his brightest because a crack's let light through.

So goes what a man knows when he burns out his tool to see beyond it, as J did. When he lets one fire pass for another by figuring that he might look to the stars to feel the ground underfoot.

J allowed the notion of a one-dimensional thing, like a continuum, like a man's path, to raise the notion of a non-dimensional thing, like a single point, like a lonely man, travelling it. Hinting higher to more dimensions should his path bend or veer. Or dare be knotted into voodoo men and given structure to walk the world. Or taken further, to slow the time it takes a man to walk around, the more complicated the pattern becomes. Then beyond, risking the notion that other wills might collide, knowing that infinite complexity is a property of nonconcentric rippling. Into the ultimate prayer that he might finally see what's really going on, implied by all the winding.

Light from the farthest star, travelling away from the beginning of time, defines the end of the space that holds it and all the nature of the space within. As it expands, as what is this universe, into what is not. Not any absence because no presence dare be suggested. No *nothing* that might suggest a *thing*. Simply into not. From which one plus any other must eventually undo it all.

J commits to unraveling the pattern that light traces that becomes men and the things they do. Only so far as noting tendency, enough to bridge the gap between spaces to finally connect man to his soul on the other side. Connect the best of both worlds to finally be able to entrust man with his own motivation to dream. He thinks he can make them understand the consequence of that. Once he's allowed himself the full expression of what he's capable, of a perfecter wording.

Until then, he explains only to strangers, only with their dicks in his hand, the shame that he's endured, forced into him from the meatside. All those terrible terrible things that he doesn't dare to try to explain to those people who love him most. *Doesn't* is like *always* only it means *never*. He never spills a word about the beauty of this moment that he spends in the putrid underbelly, an instant before he erupts from it like a geyser. The risks and the weights of it are beyond their concern, beyond their desire to understand.

Those people who love him are titans. Earthbound monoliths who'll have to be ripped to heaven along with everybody else. Or heaven down to them. They're the strongest characters in J's story because every step he's ever taken has been a step away from them. He's deeply ashamed and they've seen every fall. Those who love him most, those from whom he came, they're his strongest reference point. Who must be kept naïve, given no reason to wander, so that he'll know all the more surely when he's come full circle.

For now, he can't explain. He doesn't know how to make them receive it. How could he explain that he's destroyed what their love created? That's how they'd see it and how could he justify it? Probably only by forgiving M for leaving him alone. Let him explain. But how could he? How could he make anyone accept the moral game he'd created about a broken boy in which he risked his mortality for the chance that he might be the perfect hero and his story the perfect romance?

Surrounding M, scattered all about him, are the details of the story of how J passed whole into heaven. J has instincts about how it might all fit together. He's seen more than enough to be convinced of what he'd need to rearrange and what he'd need to forego in order to tell the story just right. He's a scavenger dragon, turning garbage into fire.

M pulled J's head heavenward by defining the hottest hell as a vector, offering scenarios to a dreamwielder in which he is and sees the sun. So J risked it, hoping that when he could finally consider the potency of the moment relative to the power of the source he'd be set free. Finally be able to see that a timeless man's shadow forks like a desert cactus. Like a desert cactus might be the light footstep of its own shadow on the sun.

For the sake of what he bore for M, J became like that light from the farthest star, shining away from the beginning of time, defining all the moments therein. He wishes he could live his days as just a knot in a beam of light.

When the man's no longer in the way, and the path of the light's unobscured, he sees entireties when he looks back. He sees that perspective is the only real distance between any two creatures. J sees their patterns in his own patterns and how it's all connected. He sees clearly past himself to remember a white speck in a black infinity.

He's been called Bodhisattva for the words he's etched on wood. His body's been decorated with the Inukshuk. He's been called Pilgrim while walking the seven years it took to reach the end of someone he deemed worth traipsing. Within a ten-year curse, which took his life then gave it back to him, leaving him to contend with a man once worth traipsing but too soon found not vast enough.

J's a pilgrim and he needs to keep walking until he finds the entrance to a cave that leads to a crystal cavern underneath the earth. To sing in a cavern made of crystal is to have the whole world hear your song. M stepped backward in time and J became a ghost to him, which will make his song all the more haunting when he finally gets the chance to sing it.

But first, with the curse lifted, he must reword what he's so far chosen. Then be wise enough or brave enough to choose again what it takes to write a happy ending. Some acceptable reason for the bad path underfoot and why he's dragged them all through it instead of walking the long way round. So that what could've been the documenting of how he went crazy becomes an explanation of higher self, changing the focus of men's eyes from the cells that comprise them to some just reason for them to see.

With which few man might be trusted for the sake of what they tend to look at. This is a sad moment for too many. So many that the balance is in that direction. The level upon which the holy war must be fought must find some way to weigh the potency of the individual somehow greater than the song of the masses. If the balance is to fully swing. Or, better yet, a balance achieved. It must be spread like some infection consentlessly throughout the world.

Seems it always comes back to that.

Knowing that heads was possible, J flipped a coin a thousand times and every time got tails. This is how he's sure that something strange is going on. It confounded him into this confusion: A random series of numbers allowed to run on forever, at some point, would generate a billion sixes. At the second to last six, if a man was asked to predict the next number he'd be a fool if he chose six and he'd be a fool if he didn't. He's a fool by his involvement in the act of guessing unless he sees above the spiral and decides to climb instead. He must then question the random nature of the generator or, if he cannot question the machine, he must question the inclination in the nature of man that he be a fool. That within some infinity there are times when a man must be a fool no matter what choice he makes should he choose to choose.

Choose to sublime into the way of things, taking heed of the treachery and the grossest fallouts of whatever might befall. A man walking a path, can hold his head down, or he can look up. It's all the same sort of seeing just different reasons and explanations for arranging. Different commitments to different roles. All different kinds of motives for a man's life amid the life he finds himself living, sailing past horizons with senses unconcerned. Or unconcerned with the sense of it at all, with what tends of the heavier things while the lightness goes on glowing, churning like a furnace with all that heat to channel.

You're either with us, or you're not. So it all unfolds.

Sometimes a child dies in a story with a happy ending. Some nights, the lover you gave your life to love doesn't come home. Sometimes, when a man finally reaches the end, he sees that there was a quicker way. A safer way. The unforgiveable can happen and a man'll feel like a fool. Or be forced to find a better way to tell the story. To learn more than the obvious lesson about how much it hurts to walk through thorn patches for the sake of a blackberry. Sometimes the real story, the real reason for the story, lies in what's left after it's all been told away.

So there's no reason for J to offer his family his condolences. But J's writing it anyway. *"I'm so sorry."* Just like he told the nurse, who waited while he cried, "this didn't just happen to" him. For the sake of that. It happened for the sake of something so much more brilliant and greater. He just had to find himself first so that he could find that next. He'd been walking backwards for a lifetime and had to reach the end before he could make an accurate estimate of his wingspan and fangsize. Before he could wander off, all honed and ready, to try to stumble upon whatever's been calling. Because he's sure he hasn't found it yet. Or that he's even begun to search. Right now, he's just spinning as the call gets louder and louder. A perfect pirouette. He tries to spin and spin as fast as he can. Fast enough to raise tornadoes, to begin to glow, to cauterize the bleeding life behind him and to ignite the one to come.

He's climbed the highest peak nearby only to find himself surrounded by other peaks as far as his eyes can see. This is, by no means, a solution rather a hint at some possible objectivity. A sense of futility to numb the cravings he no longer cares to quench. So he sits and thinks of caverns and of flight. First, he remembers, in order to forget, before he dares to dream.

15. Forgive and forget. A time happens long before it's foretold, all backwards and unwarranted to a spinning man. A legacy explains its cause while stars suck it all back into a nightsky of nameless constellations, waiting to remember. A perfect set of rationale lays unfolded, unconcerned about the details about the details about the hearts of men. Which become idols when taken from midst the man to be held in his hand. Hearts are meaty things, responsible for a man's flow, that can either pulse his life into him or bleed it out.

A thousand years ago, a day, a man's inclinations began as roots in a boy or one way or the other, depending upon his purpose and which way through time he's travelling. He has notions of ideas to guide him before the ideas themselves occur. He feels that he should be able to make more sense of things but nothing makes more sense to him than the beat of the street beneath feet meant to wander. So he leaves it all behind in search of reason, only to return to it someday, maybe with answers. Maybe just different ways of asking, tracing circles on a spherical world.

Granted enough time, depending upon the man, a day may come when he wakes lost on a circular path, having spent a lifetime naively mistaking movement for direction. Completely unaware that he's been hunted all along and that every track he's ever left has been followed.

He walks in circles, stalking his self as prey. Walking the length of each compass point, threading his path through. Lacing the tether of his lifetime through the points of a snowflake, resonating pockets of holy glasses below each distant footstep. Changing the sound of the earth. A song he learns to recognize in arrhythmias and disconcerts and senses he only senses that things aren't quite right. Before he attunes, enough to rearrange, and learns that he can move the world underneath him without moving so much as one foot at all. But it takes the suffering of time and consequence for his awareness to prove so malleable. Nor is he sure yet of what he can do. It must all unfold before it can unwind. So it goes.

Not until after all debts have been paid in full, of a wager entered into unwittingly, can any of this begin. A boy must be made brave. Then a brave boy must take a stupid step. He must be convinced or cajoled. A way must be found for him to stand somewhere where he shouldn't be able to stand, unaware of the will he'll come to wield, in order for him to wield it. Unaware, quite yet, of the lazy meat through which he'll then have to swing it, like a sword, to cut away enough to forgive what he had to endure to earn a will of his own. Beyond any clear notion why he'd ever done anything at all. Only to find out that it had to be this way. So he could find the voice, to define the god, to ask that god why it had to be this way. Hopefully, to see something greater to his cycling.

He falls into what he can only call love though the word fails as he speaks it. It cycles full circle, enclosing whole an oblivion. The metaphor's weak despite his attempts to be worthy of it. It's a shell or a cage he's speaking about. Some barrier keeping him dry in an ocean all around. When really he should crave water. And salt. Be able to dip his toe in and ripple the world.

Love's what confines him, in his body, in his days, insufficiently holding back a reservoir. Damning up the true deluge until desperation demands that he be cleansed by the series of truths that will flood the world only when a bright boy uses his brains like dynamite to achieve some acceptable compromise between the consequences of his natures.

He tries to grab at truths and other things that turn to clouds the more he's unable to want them properly. So he sits, in ways, and tries to see the world. What's real beyond what just seems it. How the heaviest pull of the ground underfoot is just the recombining of starlight and the ideas of man. Like the sway, which feels like direction, of a headstrong wind. He reaches to grab intention from insinuation all around. Some reconciliation between disparate things to be able to understand the furthest extent of wherever he might wander by understanding himself as he sits.

It takes the full conscious effort of his intellect to see beyond it. As it takes the full starburst of his heart to feel his role in its beating. To see however that pulsing might be intended and accounted for amongst all the other rippling. So his song can be discerned from the humming of all creation to explain his role in the harmony of the rest of the world.

But that takes time. And time's little more than a man's conjuring of a man's memories, which usually just amount to a bump in a brain or a knot in some flow or the culmination of a few words overlapping, spoken over a thousand lifetimes, while a spinning earth heaves mountaintops from ocean floors. As some seemingly innocuous set of events unfolds that will someday amount to all the reasons why he dances in the moonlight when the coyotes howl. Why he loves the desert and men who cannot handle their own genius.

It's his strongest urge to see into the light that shines when things begin to crack. The sun becomes some universal umbilicus and all of mankind spins, just a zygote still, considering whether or not it's ready to endure what it knows. What might come of what might happen should any two of them find a way to love each other right. Should the nature of the soul be satisfied somehow within the efforts of the skin. Should the single soul find some reprieve in the fractured realm of its every physical expression.

With the sun as his guide, each day, a man's dragged into the night. Left to fend for himself in the darkness, no longer connected to the world. To shiver the whole night through only to wake each morning a little heavier. Each day losing a little more faith in his own fire's ability to burn. Left alone to rely on blue streaks where a furnace once created. It reminds him of a different loneliness. One he doesn't want to quite remember but can't seem to completely forget. Just the sense of being one thing split and craving whatever cost might relieve that ache.

He's hacked away at by it. Told by compulsions within, and examples without, to want some fusion he can't define. An idea he can't refine past the long walk to get there, walking in circles on a spherical world searching to find his equal in order to understand himself. Or to find something worth admiring to understand how to become worth exploring. Seeing aspects of himself in the reaches of those whom he entrusts with his softest parts. As a means to let it all unwind just enough to see something beyond.

He needs to be held, when the crack opens up, so he can lean into the light. He needs some treasured brother to hold back his fires so the beacon only glows, though it has the power to inferno.

He challenges the sun in his deepest moments of alone and longing. Then he's forced to answer for it or to be punished for the dare. He's taught humility for the brashness of his zealous parts no matter how naïve whether they be meaty or clever or not. He's forced to acquiesce. To learn or somehow be taught that the sky's just an illusion in every dream he's ever had. Just a trick of the sun. So that he might come close enough to noting the ways in which he's being foolish.

If his understanding takes him far enough to see a pattern made of patterns unending then every impasse he hits will make him think to climb the walls of the maze. There's only so far a man can walk on a spherical world. It's what becomes his sense of futility, which is akin, and a guide, and a key to ascending. He stands on top of the maze wall only to see for miles that one place is as any other. He becomes aware that he's a single point within some uniform infinity, hinting at what's really going on. Suddenly he understands that all he comprises is bound into him and in him as well. He becomes a gateway to his full self across realities, climbs down and rests his body.

Maybe that's why he prefers men who cannot handle their own genius. Because the cracks between what they deem as real are vast enough to be more light than shadow. Enough to see that man *is* the veil thinning. That man need only walk through shallow puddles to appear as god.

The way clouds condense when the pressure drops. As the expanding universe stretches new matters into being. The same way that the chosen man arrives when the time is ready and enough truth exists in the collective to risk it. His braver parts must feed on his weaker ones if he's to survive the threat he poses. A scavenger Midgaard becomes adamantine, drawn from the ether to complete the design. A moment's evolution of ideas compounding can be mistaken by man for time's progression no more. He emerges as the figurehead of all that amounts to who he truly is.

He becomes Bodhisattva, the coinciding of things. If the word "thing" can be applied to no thing at all. And all the tiny horses and all the tiny men. He has to forgive these things sewn into his character as the story's explained. He must see love as the planets collide. Learn to hone his sense of the futile for the sake of being able to recognize a path worth wandering. He must will quiet to feel the will beneath it all as his own. Take breaths to sustain his animal. Hold hands long enough to vibrate but not long enough to glow. Until he can control it. He must see that he's on his own here in order to surpass his loneliness. And reverse his desire to unite, from a collapsing star, into a search for harmonies in the blinding white light.

There can be no illusion when there is no light just as there's time between a man and what he sees. He begins to understand that there's darkness immediately around him despite the outside reaching in. Under the blue sky, that's not really there, and how pretty his reflection is in someone else's eyes. What a man sees is the universe collapsing. What he senses, sewn into an imposed reality, is the destruction of everything. From the source of all around, all the information gathers into a pinpoint in his mind. He's inundated and squeezed out of existence, made dimensionless, within his senses reach. If the story's only told to him, then he's no part of it at all. Not writer, not actor, only spectator. He's only animal, if that's what he's doing. He's a rock rolling down a hill. On a planet aimed at another. Destined to be eaten by the end of time. By a timeless man's spark to genesis.

Man's purpose is to sense. Any interpretation of those senses is an abomination. But there's more to a man that a man cannot know. For all his knowledge, and his pretty little face, are just things made of meat. Man's an animated machine. Part tool, part animus, praying all his days that built into his mechanism is the hope of his release from it. That someday he'll be a real boy should he be able to refine his ability to sense down to the hushest whisper. To what he suspects of god and the paths he didn't wander. So that he can turn his power against himself, have faith enough to close his eyes and take that fateful step again. To understand that *how* and *why* can both be answered *will*.

First the gathering, now the quickening, next the life of man.

What a man *is* must travel the other way if he's to have any certain effect at all, from where he comes from, into what's going on. He must remain unconcerned with his own affectations and ripple into the world with his song and the warmth he rubs onto other things. Blindly allow his animal its sway and accept some greater way of existing in the echoes of footsteps and imprints in sands. Remarkable man does remarkable things. With his tool, he builds crystalline amphitheatres, sings where other men can hear him, be touched and begin to resonate themselves.

Man's only connected to man with light anymore. Though, ironically, it's the solid things that distract man from touching man. Solid parts cast shadows. A man must have it in him to realize this and to be brave despite the fact. He's where the light stops. He casts a shadow and might never be a part of any other man's life any more than this. Despite the cravings of his animal's call, under the moon's light, rounding the earth. Privy only to another man's greatness by assumption and an unconvincing empathy at most. So easily confused by the voices screaming. Those of his body to further his clan. Those of his heart to justify it. Those of his mind to find reason for pride. And the conflict of all those around.

He spends his days wrenching the word *man* to change its meaning from what he's been told to something he's trying to find. He looks to others. It's the first thing he does. If he's a smart man, truths collide across times and he confuses his burning desire for something that it's not. Love is seeing how a thing is justified. That's the simple truth of it. Whatever a timeless man might come to know, he has a sense of it already. It pervades his life as the subtle sense of some pull drawing. It raises no questions of god or free will because, to a timeless man, neither comes first. He simply is. And what he sees in love, he can look through, if he can, to see the real truth of what he's been craving all along. And move beyond it, toward it. Into the light, he flickers, drawn back into the source. To that place, on the other side, that he's only seen through cracks.

The power of it stuns him when he realizes that he casts a shadow. And how that shadow eclipses, more and more, the deeper his mezmer's hold, the closer he gets to the source of the light. Faced with all combinations of all possibilities combined, he sees that he's been denied suspicion. Of paths he might now take, having forgiven his own. Of pronunciations of the name of god. The closer he gets, more and more, parts of the world get darker and darker, as the heat becomes worse and worse. Until it's nearly unbearable, until he races to finally step in, out of his own anguish, into the light, a vampire drinking in the sun, ready to turn, to see it all illuminated. To finally see it all made light.

16. Made light. The veil thins. Not thin enough to tear. J won't allow it. It's enough that things seem thicker, slower. He feels like a jellyfish floating through, every ripple played on his tendrils as on strings of a violin. He's connected to everything if he allows it. If he listens closely enough to their thoughts and changes a letter here or throws a word in there until it's worded just right and casts spells.

A single will stands out amongst all the others in a moment turned to steel. One man sees his reflection and is awed. His will begins to glow like sunlight from his chest. Hot enough to make molten the steel. The mirror melts to mercury and his image merges with the sea. A man need only see how the moment reflects him in order to change the moment's nature. Subtly, at first, until he's sure he can control it. Then, when he's sure that he's free of all contradictions and saboteurs, he can dare to will in broad strokes and brilliance.

The first thing that he'll will is love. He'll will it come full circle. If he's that kind of man. When the power of creation's no longer obscured by what's been created, he'll see that there's more sense to be made within the unfolding than any he can make without. He races back into the thick of it because it's clearly his lot. Rummaging through the pile to refind the greatest thing he's ever felt. He's seen it from above, that it becomes a gateway when a man completes a fiery loop, and he's no longer afraid.

He becomes like a porpoise lured into doing backflips in the daytime, light out of water though he's no longer able to swim. Nor jump high enough to nudge the sun. Or dry enough to unfurl wings. So back to it, as with all things and the moments of freedom in between them. He dives back into his shadow, ontop his reflection, falling back into the sea.

This is always how two hearts collide. As they always will. When a man's finally himself and can answer his mindless cravings with full-imagined mind by folding the fabric between all things and diving back into it. By summoning or stumbling upon someone worth craving and by pulling that someone hard enough to bring him near, sending ripples from their ricochet to stir new momentums.

J moves ahead of the plot. Races past what took the slow path around what he decided to climb. To accelerate the slowness that he can no longer bear. He withdraws an ungiven consent with a will come of age, almost wiser. He unfurls his tendrils and turns to feel the world. He hasn't stared at it long enough but he's stared long enough to see that there's a tool and a medium upon which it's working and consequences to suffer, no matter.

So, he wakes, a thing suddenly, out of nowhere, eager to know more about how to choose how to navigate the consequences of his will without getting distracted from for what he's being prepared. He's in a race and time's running out. So he knows he's not alone. Whether it be fate or nature or another will of man. His will's not absolute in the world it inhabits. There are rules still and walls and some shepherd oracle guiding. He's a jellyfish, subject to tides, safely floating somewhere between earth and sky, belonging to both but to neither.

In his effort to will things into this world, he sees that there are clearly fixed points. Things that no solitary will can affect to change. A man's saddest times are those times when he's alone and unable to affect the world any more than a strong breeze beneath a tablecloth tacked down by plates and foods and other things that don't change when willed upon. Things a man must learn to recognize if he's to see what's really going on, who he's really dealing with, who's really there beside him and whose concerns more when concerns coincide. Or worse, conflict.

Only a sitting man can truly see that every man's where he wants to be. The worst thing you can do to a man is give him exactly what he wants. Wont is the opposite of will and thereby they're exactly the same. So J's forced to understand the wills that brought him here. He's trying to stop the juggernaut creeping. Some heavy sense of sadness keeps longing for what's lost rather than seeking something other or more. He wanted one life and got another. No matter how close he got. Now it's time to decide what to want next. If it turns out that he wants the same thing then he must seek a perfecter wording and make himself beautiful in preparation, in this meantime.

So far, he's refined a set of rules that make it easier to pick up where he's left off when he's forced to drop everything to tend to what's wandered. Or been wrongly remembered. Or stumbled. Or waivered. He repeats these rules when the night falls and he finds himself on dark streets looking to settle for any moment to happen. He repeats them when he wakes alone in the morning and has to convince himself of what half a day's worth. He repeats them now to figure out what to do next: If a thing's true on one level then it's true on every level. This is the only way that god might know man. A man has within an arm's reach all that he needs to solve whatever problem he might be facing. A man's responsible for every detail of his life, down to the weather. And, every man's exactly where he wants to be. Though some men aren't there at all. They're not there to hurt you. They're not there to suffer.

So it goes. J has a virus. This is all there is to consider right now. It's a seed, once planted, which sprouts the truth of the single path before him while bracing the reach of any detours that might come. It grows the thickest trunk and goes on to explain what branches. The path of his life is connected by predilections and dispositions, his wills, his ways, his wanders. A path drawn upward by the whims of evolving fate then forced to branch by whosoever might will it. Should any single bloom be will on a flowering thing that'll someday wither.

J has a virus. It has something to do with a sad boy's will to die. Which is really just a sad boy's wish for his sadness to go away. Because he doesn't yet realize that he's going to die either way, no matter. So he falls in love whenever he can because it comforts him and holds him at night and takes his mind off the terrible things he's inclined to want to consider. It wasn't a choice, and it isn't a choice, it's just what he did before he had a will to do anything at all. It's just what he does when he does have it. So it doesn't matter. Because his days are the price of his brilliance.

What a man does is ultimately what he is. J's proud of what he did. Proud to know how powerfully he's loved. Proud to be proven capable of it despite whatever consequence might come. Now he knows that he can walk across glowing coals. That he can make love the only thing and use it to explain everything else.

It just happens that the love J was granted had a fork in it. Two paths that led to the same place. A good path, he assumes, and a bad one. A loop in the reasons for his affections that are explained as easily as they explain, no matter, and grant a sort of perspective to a fractured boy. To two fractured boys. Then to the world if he's allowed to push back against the gathering light or if he does it anyway. If he can slip fully into his body, reverse the flow of consequence and become his own real guiding animus. His perfect image of man.

J has a virus. Because of a sad boy's eagerness to pay whatever price might afford any form of solace. He wanted solace and found it quite readily in the arms of another sad boy. One just like him in all the worst ways, both of them prone to seeking refuge in the sadness of the world. What they found together was bliss. Defined by contrasts and tricks of the mind. Though they were never any more together than two layers of skin and the speed of light would allow. The unity they suspected was only comparable to what they felt. What they felt was something entirely other. And they were too dumb to recognize it. Still, the lesson is learnt by contrast and again the moment's purpose changes.

J has a virus. He assumes for the sake of love. But he has no love any longer so the moment's purpose must then be only that he has a virus and to what end that truth might be used. Like the reflection of a wrecking ball growing in a mirror. So it falls to him and for what he's being prepared. As easily, he could've been a cripple, a fat girl, a monkey grinding or the Dalai Lama. A way would've been found to demand of each of them the discipline it takes to make real life.

Backward and forward and always in time. J sees how he's been changed. Forced to bear a deeper connection. No longer pretending within an impossible reach. He's remarkable man and the tips of his tendrils are ultraviolet. Now his only chance for love is a regardless, fearless thing. Some together he dreams of managing with some man without a face just yet. A man who'll have to be kept separate because J's ability to love is a threat now. As maybe it was all along. His ability to love is diseased. So he's learnt. To see his love more clearly, he had to have it all taken away. To see that love is too light a thing on this earth and must be bound from meaty men. From wreaking havoc. From an unknowable fruition.

J loved, first, to escape life. He's come to believe that love's the compulsion of the fractured soul of all-life seeking what was once whole before the first cell divided. An effort so easily misunderstood. He sees, in this ideology, the truth that life wants to be lived. But, first, that life must grow strong enough to be able to bear its living or must somehow be sheltered from the riptides and the gales as it floats along. Jellyfish man is quickly made aware of consequences and sensations he must then refine. He learns that some men live their life by taking life from other people. Some men simply give their own life away. Some guard the life they have and seek no more. Some give life and take it equally. They flow like earth mother jellyfish.

A man need only look to the nightsky to see that there's all of black infinity for the singleness he seeks to be realized. To realize that now's not that time. While the dreams he dreams within that nighttime are of two layers of skin and the speed of light. Until he can dream a way for his power, a power that's so far only wrecked, a way it can be made to build. The same way that light from burned out stars is slowly eaten by his eyes. Like a diamond, cut just right, that traps all the light and someday births a galaxy.

A man must become rock if he wishes to reach for air. Otherwise he flies off into the darkest night and is never seen again. Just as a man craving fire must chain himself to the seafloor and try to find some balance therein. He knows that the moon controls the tides rising up around his chin. He understands that everything he knows of the moon is just what the sun's told him. He needs to see the moon as the earth in the sky, with his feet in the water, beneath the eclipse of the sun. Standing within this alignment, he'll be made aware of his place upon the earth, sending ripples out to where the ocean meets the blue sky, staring off into where once there was sun.

There's power in the absence of the sun, as there is in its churning inferno, as there's power in certain ground underfoot keeping you from falling. Into the lava below or spinning off into the sky above. So is there worth in knowing that you're nothing more than the footstep your shadow leaves on the sun. This understanding leaves a man to go about his days lightly gleaning.

Ask a man "what do you do?" and most men will tell you what's his job. Or what his games are. He'll reveal how he sees himself and with what eyes. What you do is what you are. And what you are is what's your purpose. The key's to find the will within all of that. To use this knowledge to see that any man defined as part of some machine suggests another who might flow between the gears. Suggests a higher coiling.

So J sits and, in sitting, he feels the fabric pull. Feels all the information of the universe flowing in. He reaches to reflect or to absorb. He tries some days as a full man and other days as one filling. Until there's some sense to the rhythms of what he can do. Some surges he can amplify with a surf along a wave. Some reverse by standing petrified in their way. Some can be calmed with an opposing truth hummed just so. Some raised to tsunamis by typhoons and siren's songs.

He becomes original man. Wreaks his will like a tantruming godchild to see what stays real after he's taken his talons to it. So he can convince himself of ways to find pleasure there instead of in the places where his will's half mistaken. There's no time to go back to that kind of life. He's taken all the mistakes he's made and said them better. Said them into different truths.

Clearly unbiased, J's already said, "woe is M. And M will no more." And he's understood his place in it. It takes only the unclenching of some muscle to dispel whatever his body's feeling, knowing it's easier to suffer than it is to not suffer. Especially when the man inside knows better. J need only sigh, and let go, to get that horrible yearning out of him. To see clearly, the truth that he really was the greatest part of M's life. No matter what he remembers of those seven years. No matter what's left of them. He was a good man, on a bad path, and those days really did hold so much beauty. As far as he can tell, as much as he's been able to glean by sifting through the litter. By somehow scavenging for what doesn't seem to be there. What's only implied by its glaring absence. So it goes.

Before being fully realized, remarkable man must achieve forgiveness for the ways of things. He must accept that a child sometimes dies in a story with a happy ending. While, all the while, seeing that every story flows into every other. He must be made aware that there's a point and that a point must be made. As time's explained, it becomes increasingly pressing that he make himself more and more beautiful for what he's being prepared. By seeing deeper into what's already beautiful. Enough to become it. Enough to amplify it across levels for that time when he comes into his own wording, loud enough to ripple, knowing there are perfect ways of saying things.

Ahead of the plot, the time comes once again to test the universe. J prepares whichever part of the newt conjures great things and clears his throat.

He decides to give his book to his friend who owns the café in which this story begins. Just to accelerate things in the real world while he drifts off to imagine another one on top of it. He spins off things he absolutely cannot control to pay the balance for what he absolutely will. She's his best friend, in the sense that she knows how he's ancient, who entered his life along bloodlines to become family. Her name is L. She's the one who introduced him to M, the boy who sought refuge in the sadness of the world. She once bade him beware his curses.

17. His curses. In watching, he sought and, in seeking, found. The power of wielding despite the weapon weld. He needs to see the solid places that hold the pattern held. A man needs food and warmth and, should he love, that as well. Though the interim between his déjà-vus is all he has right to claim. Like some metal ball rolling. In some cosmic pinball machine.

J's no further along in the sense that there's nowhere to go. He's at both ends of it and spread entirely across the deserted expanse in between. At first, experience had been the motive force of the advancing plot then the words themselves began to show the way. The world's become more and less since he's decided to sit. To consider how matter gathers and to see how, and to what end, solid things draw.

While a man, chained to the seafloor, feels the water on his jaw and is unconcerned. He finds the riptide slithering around his ankles more unnerving, knowing that a strong enough current might invert a jellyfish and the whole world become his insides. The sunlight focuses through his thin-veil skin and his matters begin to glow.

J's not sure yet that he can be trusted with fire. He sees that he's been trying to convince himself with cycling absurdities and his preoccupation with self has begun to bore. He's been looking for someone who knows him. Now, he no longer wishes to be known. Now, his greatest effort is to hold his form in the unraveling. Is to refuse to be blown away to cinders by the solar wind. The heat becomes stronger, the closer he gets to the source. The easier it becomes to submit. To allow to unwind the delicate spiral of man.

He's under a barrage of attacks. His will spends each day cycling through what and why to wont. His body reflects every waiver. When he's sad, his body begins to bubble. Life, within him, sees the chance and takes it. He pays close enough attention that he can feel when the life inside him changes moods. When it's obvious that his life might be better lived and other wills battle to take over. His glands swell in his sore neck in some gesture of evolutionary obligation but he knows that the game's a different one now. Despite how tender. He's a fangless cobra doomed to swallow his own venom or to spit it at people walking by. His inclinations are explained by their outcomes and he sees that it's all just a trick of light.

There's nothing in man's world that's not just the sun's painted light. *To see* means *to understand* to a man. *To understand, to dispel.* To see the truth of a thing is to know that it's made of light. Is to watch it set on fire by the seeing. A man's awareness is like a magnifying glass. Should he be found brilliant, when studying a thing, then that thing's suddenly across a focusing lens from a white-flamed inferno. Is to feel the glare of the eye of the sun.

The sun's the one constant across all men's realities. The godsun, the godlight, bound by the spiral into everything and men's lives. It's the locus, begun to tear, of the harmony of the scrutiny of all of mankind. It's where a singular truth unfurls, untangling an unraveling pattern in tendrils of wisping light. The truth that, when bound into any pattern, an omnipotent thing is no longer what it is. The sun was once the center of men's universe. It won't be long before it comes full circle.

J's watched it come full circle three times already as he's been sitting. He sees it in the story he's telling and all the worlds he's watching. As the ideas, he has, occur. He refused to go on but that didn't stop a thing. So he has to twist it. He has to wade through chin-deep snow to find some morsel to graze on. Like bison in Yellowstone in winter. There are more fixed points, now, tacked down and he's bridged the distance between more than a few of them. He's grown fatter in his certainty and the fabric's beginning to constrict his chest.

His heart races at the notion of suffocating. A psychic once told him that he'll die that way. He will stop breathing. He will be absorbed by some other element and be cut off from the air. This didn't surprise him and he nodded. He's always assumed that he's going to die in the ocean. His lovers always leave water bottles behind for him. He always dreams of rivers and lakes and seas. Someday he's going to live on a sailboat and take it to Antarctica. Because he's just as afraid of the cold as he is of the water, which is why he practices holding his breath while he worships the sun.

He wants to call into the world for someone's will, no matter its translation, to choose him. Someone on his path or someone who'll welcome him on his. Any parallel life he'll fit into. Because he can't bear the thought of leaving this place cold and alone. Terrifying winters have beset him more than once when he's been denied his right to sun. He's been told, by his yoga cult best friend, that the last moment of a man's life is the most pivotal one. The culmination of the phenomenon of that. He's been told that a man's last echoing thought is what becomes his afterlife. The place where he'll spend what remains of time before all the wills once again coincide and absolve.

J ails when he sorrows. Or he sorrows when he ails. Either way, he ails and sadness and sickness tumble with his inability to note which comes first. He needs only to realize that his sadness and his sickness are connected and that both are best avoided. He's stunted by an incredible sadness, sometimes, that he can usually only barely find a way through. And it's getting harder. When no single star is visible for the sake of the black of the night. Which is unforgiveable and can only last so long. Once a man finds something truly infinite, whether it be darkness or blinding white light, he either succumbs to it or he finds his purpose therein. He sees that there's some place within infinity for every combination of possibility. He sees the eventuality of miracles.

So back to it. So it goes. He has only this world, this meantime, and he has to know this world if he's to be safe in it. If he's to keep others safe. He must find a way to call out to his own brilliance, and to have it respond, if he's going to be ready when it comes time to leave it all behind. By which, he means to dive deeper down in.

On some mountaintop, someplace he's already been, the forest below looked like moss and all of the men looked like mites in it. He's seen the naked earth, the bleeding earth and places where his echoes have made cavern walls begin to glow. He's been to the White Swan and waded through Grendel's waters. All the time expecting to meet his counterpart in places where they were both clearly alone, seeking miracles. Most times you find yourself in places you absolutely are not.

Barefoot in the blowing grasses, in the hottest midday sun, a man walks to the center of a wavy field. He takes off all of his clothing and lays face down in the grass. He gathers what he needs of stillness and reprieve then plants his hands on either side of his body. A deep inhale raises his chest from the ground to perfectly arch his back.

He's split up the backside from the soles of his feet. One foot takes a left step and the other a step right. It's this sort of indecision that's torn him up the meridian. Why he drags his legs behind him when he pushes his chest up off the ground. He rolls forward over his toes until the soles of his feet face heavenward. A sigh is his bay at the sun. He seeks the perfect curve with his body, from toe to crown, because energy's a thing that spirals and he wishes to be the perfect conduit, even though he's cracked from his ass to the base of his skull.

His muscles wrap like ribbons around the bones that hold his form. The muscles thicken, around his legs and calves. His ass tightens to two perfect loaves and puckers. Two guy-line muscles raise his torso to cup the sun, like a drawbridge, tied taut to a back that's rippling. A sheath of dimpled muscle bunches, like furled wings above his ribcage, about his perch, upon his shoulder's blades. The sun's warmth on his face, when he stares into the sky, is the same warmth draped across him while he prays with his cock in the grass.

He moves before he thinks to do it, and clenches. He rolls back over his tiptoes, lowers his head from the sky and raises his hips from the ground to reverse the arch. He opens his asshole to the sun, dragging his cock behind. Hanging, in midair, he feels the breeze across it. He holds this pose as the strain builds. As he strains to channel what the sun's let him hold. He kicks one leg forward on the pivot of the other, careful to manage the balance. His cock dangles in the split. He imagines a lover there to lick a drip of sweat. This makes him hard as he raises his arms off the ground and stretches to reach for the sun. Lines explode as meridians, delineating the meats and the man. All clenched and bracing, his full erection points to the sky. It drips a drop of sweat onto the folded grass.

This is what it's like to exist as freewill. To never again suffer rule or confine. It takes the full discipline of will to hold the poses. Full acrobatic will to never touch a real thing again. So much discipline to a man who feels he's losing it. Trying to hold onto a thing, flailing not to be held, when really he should just let it go. Let it loose to do its worst so he can have a free hand to pull at threads and no longer wonder why it had to happen, what was done, or what he did, or whatever, to understand the man he loved. And how surely he understands him now that they are brothers.

He must find any way to deal with what refuses to bend. These fixed points all tacked down. Or he can accept that he can reach no further. Feel the extents of his form and work instead to stretch his tool. Make efforts to become more aware of the muscles he'll need to dance more gracefully between his consequences. To never have to touch anything real for longer than it takes to ricochet. He's confined by whatever spiral he's spiraling and the game's not as fluid as he's imagined so far. He's of a sect, of a clan, worshipping ancestors. This is the distance between him and the next thing. It's the final piece put into place. He knows now that he cannot be made to feel. So he learns to take his time, no longer worried.

As he reaches for the sun, his hard cock lightly raises. He senses for the ground more surely to brace himself and to maintain his balance. He thinks of a tree. He gathers whatever strength he can as he reaches further than his body allows, convinced that he's somehow reaching beyond it. That's all it takes to note the distance between him.

He can't resist the strain for long. He lowers his torso slowly over his front leg, puts his hands to the ground and slides his leg gently back. Then he lowers himself to the ground. The grass is warm and yields. He closes his eyes as he lies against the planet that holds him as they hurl through space. He calls it brother and laments before he returns to being man. He takes a deep breath in through his nose, pushes his chest off the ground then pulls his legs up under him. Kneeling, he leans forward and drops his forehead to the ground again without intending to, simply craving any sort of being held.

As tree roots take nutrients from the earth and water and strength. He feels he could be a flower again. Plant his face deep in the darkness underground while his softer parts and petals wander in the wind. He's sure that man was flower once before he swapped his fires. Before he pulled his head from the darkness of the solid earth, forsook stable ground and lost the balancing sun.

A tree takes nutrients from the earth and water and strength. Its leaves breathe in air while feasting on the sun's fire. It needs no mitigating mind to serve its purpose. Man must decide when to take nutrients from the earth and water and strength. Though he breathes without a thought of it and makes light into lives. Clumsy clay-man reaches to catch butterflies with boulders. The light that simpler creatures feed on comes to him as information and stops there, in his doe eyes, while he considers. He emerges as a pattern, as a nexus, in the white noise from all around. So goes self, what he senses and what he mistakes for choices he might decide to make.

So man's mostly stupid because he's simply awed, knowing that every decision is an act of god. He sees the light gather to become the world around him. From that world into this one. He sees how the light's bound into the world and into him as well. In seeing it, he feels the touch of the hand of god. Or remembers having felt it.

A tree is a bridge from land to ether. A tree takes the power of the godsun to gather its form in the solid world. Man's a different bridge altogether with no strong hold in either firmament. Too distracted by the chance to choose that he can't see, for all the indecision in between, how his story's already told. When finally he comes into his true nature, he's used to a lighter way and must learn how to navigate what's heavy. By daring to pull at certain threads and by realizing that some cannot be reached to pull. Until his will's stronger than the consequences of his will.

There it is then: The bridge of man. Man's a loose thread dangling. The one thread, if pulled, which unravels it all. He's capable of god's will and must be held trapped in this interim for the threat he poses. He should lower his head and walk with his head down. For fear that he might see something beyond him and feel the need to reach for it. The more a man heads toward something, the more it becomes possible. No man should be trusted with that. Until he's fully able to translate. Until he can become, or find someone to sit with, for whom that means exactly that.

18. Exactly that. J taps his fingers on the table at a café, trying to word something just the way it's worded right. An obsessive somewhere near him counts each tap. She believes he has to make it to a perfect hundred or something horrible's going to happen. He stops at eighty-nine to write something perfect about a river and she doesn't kill herself that night.

In the same way, someday, someone will approach you and say, "your words have profoundly affected my life." The music in the background will crescendo and all life will go on differently. J smiles when he thinks this and marvels that there might be versions of what's really going on, governed only by a man's ignorance of aspects that might conflict. To see a man's reality as any set of non-conflicting truths makes him laugh. Because it's true that you can't make someone feel. But it's also true that you can reword the feelings they already do.

Just as there are certain people with him everywhere he goes. People who have varying versions of his own goings on. Those people who've grown into him or him over them. Like a cannonball rusted into the trunk of a tree growing near the gates of a fortress.

He's accepted this as his path and no longer resists the flow. The absence of his connection to water means that he must be fully bound to it. He knows that a man who cannot harbor life must be in complete harmony with his environment. Must its ebbs and flows. He's drunk it all and must now learn to take his time. While the river's guided through the land it scours.

J remembers everything he's ever written. Everything he's failed to understand in the screaming of it and gone on to plagiarize again and again. With the scribbles on his hand that he writes while walking stoned in foreign places and the words he wakes to, humming. He's trying to forget everything else until there's nothing else but the story he's becoming.

He wonders if this should scare him. And a big black crow flies past the window. But he's found that he's crooked at the base of his spine and this is more a concern to him than the magics he wreaks willingly. He's been made aware of a fine line and that he stands beside it. He's asked "why me?" Then answered. Which is more than most can say. The answer was acceptable, insofar as it made no difference, and the outcome has so far been bearable. So everyday's been dealt with. He'll maintain this and work on that to appease the sentry's eye. But he's been made keenly aware that something else is going on. And he knows it. Something else entirely.

Some suggestion he hasn't refined past the memory of having sensed it. Things he's noted while rushing past to deal with more pressing things now dealt with. Things that don't matter when running to save someone who cannot be skirted from his doom. Things of no consequence at all. Watchers in treetops just watching. Songs they sing in wind gusts and timeless convergings. Things that mean things beyond what things they mean.

A man, in a car, pulls up to a stop sign. At the same time, a man, in a car, pulls up to a stop sign beside him. They're listening to the same radio station. To a song about a man, in a car, pulling up to a stop sign.

It's time for prayers again, having found a god to pray to. J's found god. The only one he's ever found but he doesn't know where. He cannot say when or how. Nor does he care to. Not while the sentry's lurking. The demi-urge intent on denying man rapture. J's not even sure he has time to greet the foundling let alone ask him for guidance. His history is aging him again too quickly. The drop of black that greys the white is the passage of time, discoloring man and his efforts with impurities. Dimming the parts that glowed the brightest.

The last time J sees M, for a very long time, is at a bar. M hasn't shaved or cut his hair since August when J asked him to leave, since September when the psychic said he would finally go and he finally did. He looks like a sick sick crazy man, prowling for sex or any kind of touching to take life from. Clearly, rules only apply to shards of him anymore.

M smiles, quite clearly as show for J, though J refuses him. Refuses his presence, refuses his draw, refuses the consequences of not refusing him entirely. Which doesn't explain why he can't get the trembling to stop. It started in his legs and worked its way from the foundation. Rattling him. Or why he can't catch his racing heart for the beat of it.

In these convulsions, J sees that M is still his god. Only, now, so is he. J's taken the best parts of him. Left him dethroned and a mortal.

An acquaintance of J's greets him with a kiss. This man has two red spots on his face from a virus in his blood that's made him prone to red spots and greeting old friends. J's too preoccupied to notice at first and absently kisses his cheek where the red spots are. When he notices the spots, he silently recoils, makes note that he's touched the dirty heathen where he's been marked. Positive contact: unknown strain exposure. So it begins that night, what with the phlegm he hasn't been able to hack out of his lungs for months. Combined with all the trembling.

Suddenly, never before has J known a fear like this. It takes and shakes him. He scrambles for anything solid to hold onto. He sees versions of himself in the lives of the people all around him. Beginning with red spots and on to their every cliché. How totally scared every one of him is. How totally scared to see what he saw but cannot say to name. This thing that answers his tremblings and, as suddenly, stops them. What he cannot see clearly through the shaking of the moment. That thing that he saw in M's being there.

"What I am. What I am. What I am." He says it again and again. Like he spends the rest of the night writing the word *"scared"* on napkins and scraps of paper and down his wrist until he's written it enough times to see that he's really writing *"sacred."* The world's different somehow he's yet to settle into. He knows he has only himself to survive. Even though no one gets out of here alive.

J doesn't look. He knows what he would see if he did. If he bothered to look directly at M. That his smile has nothing to do with him. He'd see that M's fallen into a soft light. He's in a loop for as long as each day holds, believing that someday soon it won't. What M feels is what death feels like. In his chest, a tremble, J feels the truth of this and he sees himself as the holy ground upon which his version of this battle will be fought. He fears he's gone insane. Or that he's going to have to. With that feeling that's there now. The one, oh god, he hopes goes away. This peace with things that he sees on M's face. This attending surrender.

Just J and his smoldering angel god anymore in a bar full of people. The lonely burnt out angel he's left alone to rekindle. M once pleaded that he couldn't do it alone. And he can't. You can see him dying. Just look at him. Just a smoldering angel god and the boy who drenched out his fires. Who doused his flames with the last of his waters to see the false source of his light. Who turned away just in time before falling to cinders himself. Managing just a char. Just a singeing.

It sends him tripping, once the trembling's gone. He knows something now that he's yet to realize. He hears himself talking like a crazy person to a boy who's called him "genius" in the past. A boy who followed J home one night after M had been taken home by a gnomegoblin and J had no real choice between ways to lament what goes on in the night, with or without him. The sexual lives, of the boys he knows, fester. J kissed the boy who called him genius twice, and touched his cock, before he fell asleep.

Alone, but not alone, afraid to be scared, J decides to send one letter into the past and one into the future. But that's neither here nor there.

J spends the rest of this last night with a friend in an empty rail station until the sun comes up. This last night that he'll see M for a very long time. She spins music while he scribbles down these things to get them out of his head. To see them and call them saboteur. If the term applies. She offers an exchange of rhythms. Her beats replace his tremblings as he searches for sigils in the words his mind cannot let go.

Scared. Sacred. Holy ground. And all the other things he sketches through liquors and reefer-glazed eyes.

"I am holy ground," summons a chameleon when spoken aloud. The sun ripples from the desert ground like an invisible ocean up about the cacti and prickly things. Here, for some reason, everything seems clearer. It takes a hot hot sun to lift a fog. He feels the need for the desert heat. J sees this and sets his mind to find ways to change the color of his skin. In the sun, or in the sun's light, wherever he can find it. The desert, where the heat is and the naked earth basks. So he can learn to blend into the background. Bide time enough to rewire his brain to process images from independent eyes.

As he writes, the pages flip frantically like feathers on a wing until something takes to flight. This is sacred ground. This space where the story is told. This pen in his pocket that he's never anywhere without. And the spilling of things from imaginings to words on a page. To be imagined by somebody else. To continue that feign between men of the simultaneity of it all.

Scared scared. Sacred sacred sacred. Red red red. He's never seen the world turn red. When it turns green, that usually means that a man has witnessed a truth about the darkness. It makes the contrast between things crisper. When it turns blue, a man has seen more of the light. It drags him off beyond his senses range to see and shows him something more. Yellow happens when things just begin to glow. He's afraid to see red. It's a prophecy of fire.

He wonders if this has gone so far that he believes himself a seer. Searching for messages in altered states somewhere between rhythms and tremblings. A seer enough to see red? To be seared by it.

Déjà vu. He sees that he's set this fire before. Faster this time, he's come full circle. And on and on. He's taken to gathering, in the midday sun, the ways in which he's inclined to sublime. He's afraid he's gone crazy too. He wants to go with him but J doesn't get to lose control. Not like M. Lest his need to sublime take over and complete its life's work to end him.

M's a terrible person. He used to say that to J, every so often, and then laugh a vile laugh. That's where they met, both trying to be people. Now J understands the context of the word, how it scratched the throat when coming out. He sees how the laugh could've been *ridiculous* mistaken for *vile*. He sees that M's not a real person at all. He's terrible at it. He's no man. And there was never any hope of it at all. Not before, not during or after, all the places J was loathe to have to go to find him. To bring back whatever was left, to try to make it better. He tried everything and watched each trial fail in turn. Even tried to drug him into what he was disinclined to be. Until he was finally revealed as No man.

Once made different, some people don't get to change ever again. They're the same, no matter the Russians chasing them or the depth of the submarine they ride through any downtown urban metropolis. Through any number of the unbroachable realities, M to J is the most terrifying thing there is, an innocent evil. J's seen him feed and be fed on.

He's an unmedicated schizophrenic whose every delusion begins with his rotting. Or soon enough cycles through it. Which then drags him through unnavigable worlds on the backs of his plagues of consequences. Along with anyone who might be chained to him. He must submit to it nimbly, for just one more second, to annoyingly skirt once more the familiar face of his doom. That's the kind of creature he is and the games he's inclined to play.

J's seen M's fixed points of character. He spent his time searching for markers in the vast unnavigable meat between them. That absence in M's character that J fought so hard to understand only to find that something really is missing. Traits of strong character either forgotten or forsaken all for the sake of that. Everyone who's ever loved M is now waiting for him to die. Which is enough to sustain a creature of spite and venoms. While he goes autistic with his dying and refuses any wills that aren't man enough to take him directly there. Although J sees, in a sigil, an early autumn dust.

That's exactly that. J's alone with it. As he was alone with M when they were together. Fed and fed on, according to whichever instinct won. Each raised to be something other than he was, then discovering. The common ground upon which they met was, for each, the land of No man.

J resolves his will to never be as alone as M. Which should be enough, in his understanding of things, but doesn't entirely explain why he's too afraid to sleep that night for fear of the world he'll wake to tomorrow. Instead, he devotes his sleepless parts to considering exactly that.

The fool who walks the path to become a genius follows a path chosen by a fool. Though it hardly matters. Any path, walked long enough, leads a man full circle. It's enough that they're on the same continuum. Anything can be infinitely subdivided beyond all meaningful reason to. The same can be said for the path of a man's life. A man either succeeds or he tries.

J could've been anything in men's world. He's smart enough and beautiful and capable of brilliant insights. Instead, something else was chosen that none could name to call him. Something before them and after and into the deepest parts of their moment. He might not have noticed had he not been rapped on the skull and forced to cower, to cocoon himself in a pocket of null space where the consequences from other realities couldn't ripple into his own. For his perfect understanding of chaos and men's hearts, his only concern must be the experience of one man in the violent experiencing of now. As it explains them all.

He devotes himself to hunting perfect moments.

19. Something else to think about. Life keeps on happening whether a man resists or accepts or involves himself in its flow. This is the truth of it for someone who believes reality flexible, someone who's seen reality bend through his own eyes or the eyes of any one of the creatures that he traps and cages. Those he works his way into, until they're one of the many suctions on his tentacles unfurling. He can use them, once he knows how they feel, knowing that man is the world changing.

J used to be a fat kid. He's watched his body change the more he's grown into it. The more he's understood the use of the reflection of man. How the world's inclined to change like a slideshow, offering a keen man perspectives between the flashing images of his life. What once took years, over these last numbered days, has taken only his will be done. J's sometimes by a million little wills directed.

Slabs of meat, by sinews, tethered together. A million little pieces of a million smaller creatures, clinging to a framework of solid rock. While time wanders and small creatures forget themselves. As function grows from happenstance to become the ways of life. The air changes and the water and the land to suit the physics of a thing unfolding. New needs demand new organizations. So higher order arranges and reason gets confused for purpose. Muscles act out wills of animals whose needs wander while time wanders. And singular thoughts arise.

A million minds thinking singular thoughts. This notion raises and J sees that the world must be different now. Since, quite clearly, the time has come. His dreams are too vibrant lately, both intimate and foreign, in which he finds subtle signs that hint what they do not tell. Hint at something J's been dreading and preparing for. Something he can no longer keep from trying to explain. He's to focus attentions, all of his perspectives, because he has to be ready.

He's not afraid anymore. Finally, he's excited by what all of this implies. All he's gathered from a consistent glare at the thought of No man and all men. He's watched worlds evolve from his perch atop the mountain he climbed to get there. Seeking gods and settling for a cave near a bonsai tree once he breeched the clouds. When he finally felt the sun and knew the need to go no further.

He's been paired with No man for whatever the reason and whatever the result. Neither of which matter until after the meantime. When the true price of it can be weighed. He's seen the part of the cell that binds. Now he watches, knowing that any chain of reason after reason accumulates an order unto itself. Builds structures like antennae, like men, bringing order to the things they can do and tend to. He waits for the first man to conclude it. To find, within his being, room enough for a soul. J watches for something like an arm from a cloud, or a hand from a tangle in the treetops, like Thor reaching out for his hammer.

If his counterpart is No man then that leaves, for him, everybody else. He understands this without thought. He sits above the clouds on a mountaintop, having conversations across the sun. Every thought he's concluded, every artifact unearthed, is some part of what he wants to say to the world about how he spent his time here. While No man keeps his secrets. Both dreaming things they've only ever dreamed before.

No matter, everyone or no one, J's different for having arrived here. He walks into the world with a heart nearing certainty. He's suffered an unmatched tragedy. This is how he's spent his life. There's not a person like him in all the world. That he's seen anyway. Who's a knight, in a fairy tale, like him, enchanted. No one who would forgive him for trusting a blind oracle. Or for following it toward a shame that he dares describe as honor. No one who would follow his idiot path had he not gone first and bid them come.

He's different now. All sensitive to everything he could barely sense before, for the clatter. He's grown a tentacle from his left shoulderblade and he's growing used to the new senses it brings. Though he's not sure and he dreads making truth there. Biological truth of the spell of different when combined with the will to unfurl. There it is then. So close now. What it takes to contain such a furious power and what effort it'll take to control.

In his dreams, J's been told to start hunting humans. Now he's beginning to understand that he must become ravenous and vigilant. Going over and over what he made and what he can make of it. What unraveled and was all light, bound into that. Which became now and how he goes about things. Once implied by contrasts and absences, rearranged, now made prey by what wishes to predate. By all that remains as only memory of a once-living once-vibrant thing that never really existed at all. Was only dreamed of. That wreaked such a wake.

No matter the jackal birth, the thing born was living and had the chance to know life. So there is both blame and guilt here.

J's made that, which was of the utmost importance, of no import at all in a life created rid of it. If life is still what a man decides to seek after having it all willed away. Having given it all away as dowry before a glow that blinded. J did it to learn what remains when the man's finally willed out of the way. To find truth finally malleable enough to expect into life, and out of it, all of its experience.

He sees that the only way to make it bearable is to let go. He must hasten the eventual alone by no longer resisting. It was a lesson not clearly taught between two men, not nearly learned. One man who would hoard what the other would squander. Hope. So white a thing that it conjured black when both were blinded. One man left to covet the last glowing cinder of it, too afraid to look away. The other unable to see what he's looking for, too afraid to look away. While all that was lost and unseen went on regardless.

One truth for two men to be extended to them all.

J sees that the only way to make it bearable is to let them all go. Now that he can't have them. Or save them. Because he's different now. Will always be only cells apart. On one level.

Once he'd lost the right to love, the one man he gave all his life to love, he was left with only No man. Who is No man to be left with? When he's at your side but he's not there. He's alone. As they were both alone when they were together. No longer men now, each of them, something different than he was before. So a step must be taken. Either one step back or one down deeper.

For a thing to change is to see it age and to be aged for the sake of seeing it. It's the promise of absolution. To watch it change, into what it changes into, is to note its pattern. Is to find hope of something eternal in the cycling, regardless of what's caught in the sway. To find reason for change is to take into yourself an irrefutable logic and to begin to mutate in the sun.

In the combination of oblivion and all-possibility, J seeks more than just negation, annihilation. A concept beyond simple addition that leaves a man arranging obsolete ideas to nullify every mistake he's made. To make himself No man so he can begin to resonate, enough to amplify, to act as a beacon begun to glow. Halfway between what's real and what's not, a middle-ground weigh station on either side of the sun.

Once made No man, he must remain No man. He cannot forget enough to be made simple again, either way in time. He no longer fits inside a man's hold. Instead, stands mostly outside of himself and just a bit behind. He must choose to touch things that matter.

No man has the choice. He can choose to take life. In fits and fevers, he can race to quench what's insatiable. Or he can choose to make life and all life will be amplified. The idea sewn into this archetypal antihero is the conflict of a coexisting will to destroy and one to create.

Something about the combination of creation and destruction recombines in J's mind's as he plays silly games. He notes it but it's truth stands just beyond him. So he forgets it for a time and calls upon other senses. Allays the waving hands and searches deeper logics.

He stands and feels the stretch of his form. J's been doing all the right things to find himself, where he is, and to take care. He has to take control. His lungs have been his latest concern when it comes to how prone he is. First it was fits and fevers then the crawl of the microbes inside. In his faces, in his lungs. The festering in his chest he's been heavy breathing to breathe out. And all the other sorts of fleshiness that are no match for the man inside when the man's finally ready.

He's been doing a regimen of choreography and conducting, living sculpture and dissonance. He's found his templar body holy ground, a rope bridge across a chasm, heading to and away from the sun. He walks to it, the long way round, leaving markers so he'll know if he comes full circle.

He stands and feels the stretch of his form. It starts in his calf just below his knee where one of his latest dance moves has exceeded his form and changed it. This is the key to the only door he's ever found on his own, without a man in the way of his trance ending. That a man might stretch, to know the extents of himself then will the stretch beyond. To change. To bear perfect witness. As a man sits plainly with his animal.

His body's becoming as beautiful as he can imagine it. With his head held down, feeling within his senses reach to stretch what would hold him. He dances to shake loose of it for just a time. So he can see how it might be draped and to drape it more elegantly.

The stretch radiates up his leg. He reaches into the sky with one hand and the struggle in his fleshes slides. He closes his eyes as it rolls up the back of his ass, up the small of his back, over the ripple of his ribcage, past the meat of his shoulder, up, further up and away. He's raveling man. Part of what flows that cannot be resisted. Or what can be resisted but doesn't matter. Raveling man and unraveling man are the same thing, just traveling different ways through time.

Which explains why two men, so totally together, can be so completely alone. It's the separateness sewn into all being, no matter what passes for a will to unite. That wall of distinctness that J's thrown himself against till bloody. Which is just an echo of the end of time. When time has gathered all the pieces of its most complicated experiment, after happenstance has fully unfolded and collapsed, and spiraled finally out of being, into the one absolving soul of us all. Alone, or something like it, in a lonely eternity, or something like it.

Into an infinity, in a black timeless empty, in which he might find strength enough, or reason, to will another fracture. Just to forget the anguish of what's implied by a solitary moment. For the sake of parts made amnesiac to experience again, for the first time, what it might be like to be whole together. To find a love, and to love an equal, and to find some way to justify it all. Before the price unfolds and is found too high, too late, by a creature too naïve to decide. Who decided anyway and chose to pay, to surf consequence full circle to reason then to veer. In his own playtime for the gods. Like the one J already created then fell tempted into again. His very own faery tale.

20. You understand it's changed. An urge to gather is the first sense to coalesce out of the vastness. The first sense to stir out of the only thing. Given all time, in all direction, absurdities behave in strange ways. They do unexpected things with prime numbers and probabilities. Until eventually, from out of the absolutely impossible, something like fear braces itself.

Stands firm against the notion of chaos or the thought of unlikelihoods in some eternity. And the promise, implied by the sense of heaviness that follows. When what doesn't matter begins to matter, from nowhere across a ball of fire, down through the sky into man's world. Implying man and the certainty that it's not going to be this way for long.

A wind shifts. Parts of the cloud spread while other parts get denser. Patterns emerge in the dissonance, immeasurably far apart. Separated so perfectly with not a thing in between them. Then there are things suddenly, like raindrops, which begin to drip, to fill a yawning nullspace. Things pulled into being by the outrageous lack of themselves. The audacity sparks a flash of lightning. Godforms and castle cities are revealed in the flash before a looking eye.

While white long dismal clouds gather, from a sleepless slumber, and begin to look for anything to do. Small balls begin to roll when up defines itself and the urge to gather causes collisions. The sounds of which make it harder and harder to think of any way through, to get from one side to the other, unscathed, unaffected by the ricochets or consequences or the will to turn to stone.

What seems like order emerges. What's really no more than the chance for it. Order proposes function. Reason pretends purpose. A dolphin, in a second flash of lightning, tears a hole in the sun. Which has something to do with either fight or flight and an eye, not formed yet, holds the moment. For the sake of the image, it summons up the chance to see.

The absence of will is enough to conjure the possibility of it. As a cloud, gathering into pockets, gathers pockets into stars, then stars into constellations until the force is strong enough, or is still too weak, to tend big things into bigger things. Until big enough things go nova. For the chance that stardust might gather into cells, in an organ, in a man, of mankind, on a planet, beneath a star, in some other kind of man's constellation.

So comes the third sense, the sense of life's direction. Something about inevitability and the continuity of time as it pertains to the uses of things and why. Why a mountaintop would gather and rise up on a world of rain drops. Possibly for the sake of all the lures and snares of higher ground. All the things that hydrogen does that common minds mistake for intent or the hand of god.

Gravity gets confused with love. It drags a beaver into being and rolls it down the hill to build a home in a puddle. While the sight of something falling hints at the chance to jump from peak to peak. Calls an eagle into life and aims it at the sky.

As the idea of dimension takes a path, from any that might be walked, and knots the twine of it into voodoo men who stand up against the earth and take to wandering, looking to find any sort of creature who might fit into their weave. Feeling certain that they're just as inhabitable. That someday soon one of them will be able to find whatever it is about the fire that lets there be faces in it. As there are expressions in the space between the crystal and the sun's light. He'll be able to teach the rest of them about whatever it takes, no matter the broken tool, or the empty vessel, to be able to find room.

To find means to know where a thing is. As *to find* means to establish a fixed point in a timeframe unfolding. Like the heart of the sun and the direction of a man's life in reference to it. Should he notice it in time. No matter. Whether he comes from the light or is drawn into it. Or what just looks like it. Which is probably enough. What he finds as the same curious aspect to the same curious creatures popping up all around him. Into those men who go about their days with room enough to consider things like the heart of the sun or the sight of other such men considering.

Made primal by the power of it, they'll be drawn to one another. Coalesce in a dismal cloud and find an unknowable satisfaction in the gathering. Never fully able to know what it means to crave for the sake of the compulsion. Only sure of the force compelling them toward whichever thoughts begin to matter. Like all the things that it takes two men to do. Any playing house or wedded bliss that could not exist if they weren't already terminally apart. Or what one man can do, not chained to any other, in a living day with angels ascending. To or from the light, depending upon a man's perspective and which way through time he flows.

Whether or not he's found his purpose and is able to channel a greater source for the thrill of bearing it. As he goes about every effort to reclaim the spiral and to draw strength from it. To finally find any way to be able to bow to the sense of alone and live within it. Accepting that each of us must be kept individual amongst all the other expressions of the only thing if this moment is to exist at all. Man must seek to find anything worth exploring in an experience still bound by the memory of the dark entirety from which it fled. By becoming a million disciples to a softly resounding echo. Struggling for discipline enough, usually by contrasts, to hold life against its sway.

Strange that alone should be what binds us. When it's not uncommon for a man to kill himself for love. The loss of one man, by any other, might take the finding of a god to bear. And, even still, only mostly. So, until then, he must take hold of all the threads and knot each one into a tight tapestry. Light each corner's fire and ask for original help. Since he's seen the extents of himself and stretched to reach beyond. To be finally worthy of the chance to cross over.

He's Bodhisattva. His crown is to the sun as he walks through his shadow. Knowing that to walk away from a thing is the same as to come from it. Differing just in matters of perspective. Though a man must first burn a glitch in his mechanism to be able to see beneath things, to their purpose. Or just their use. He must learn to actively react to the world if he's to define himself within his freetime. Enough to chance upon the things he thinks he wants to explore. Enough to pick them out of the bright white light.

J bears the eclipse at the nape of his neck for the promises he's made and shattered. Things he saw, ten years ago, but couldn't find himself deserving. In a boy named L, spelled backwards. J beseeched the universe for some celestial sign only to have his wish twice granted. The one he would then forego. Hastening a swift and brutal ten-year curse that would suffer him false love and much worse. A curse denoted by patterns of ones and threes. Ten years ago, three years ago, one year… until the second it crosses and is over. That black hole J wished into the sun as proof of some reason to follow. What he could only follow the wrong way through time so that it seemed like he was walking away from it. Toward something shining just as brightly even though a million miles further away. No matter. Either way, he's on a path that begins and ends, or cycles somehow through, the need for the proof of god.

Or any other sign or reason that might make room for a concluded enlightenment. One that a man must be found worthy of. Since a timeless man can have tentacles long before he grows them or grows accustomed to them. He'll be distracted by their hum until he does. Long before he learns to control them or learns which currents control their sway. So he can muster the strength needed to endure one step after another and place himself somehow inside the flow.

Should a boy, born all knotted up, become a man within sight of fancy, before he's been untied and shown his tendrils, he'll be lost to their pull for a while. Drunk by the power of what it feels like to have lines spinning around him. Vectors defined by each tentacle's reach, from around his back in arches. He'll feel like he's floating in a field of dandelions, which will hint, to him, that he's drowning. As it hints, to him, of will.

For a while, he'll flail. Even though he builds perfect things. This man who's good at everything he does. Even if he should fail to realize that the price of creation is destruction, because he's drunk with the taste of it, the tide of consequence still swells. Until that moment when his attention lapses and the reservoir becomes a deluge. No matter his talents, or what he thinks he's suffered, it's not easy to be living man. This is hard. He punches the wall. Even though he bleeds and screams to god.

This shows only that he's a vessel, that he can be filled. So he waits. Though there's no such thing as waiting. Only the idea of the moment and that it might be twisted from the moment it is now. A song heard sung, humming waves to crescendos, as thoughts of it ripple through the world. On tentacles and the men attached to them. While they go about bringing souls to all mankind.

So, soon, everyman begins to understand the nature of the only moment. He begins to understand that he's only ever known one moment. All the stories that manage to explain it and not conflict. Even though there's a time in between. When Bodhisattvaman reaches into mankind with one of his tentacles to show man how he might make room. From the inbetween time, between men who have them and those who do not, to a time when all mighty men have souls.

To connect them in a sense of rippling by synchronizing the experience of all men. By shoving a tentacle in to explain away the ringing from the ricochet of his first attempt with meat. And the sad lonely somber that followed. Which sang to him the saddest song in echoes of a voice alone. A song he soon learns that they're all singing in violent harmony.

First, he tries to quiet the sadness of a lonely song by hearing the million voices singing it. By listening for it, knowing that quieter vibrations are more soothing and will grant a man the chance to look for patterns in the flows implied. Then he can lean back into it and let the current sway.

Feeling into all those around. Feeling through them once he can float freely with all of his life behind him. Seize into his very being the notion that the balance between creation and destruction can only be shifted by will, as an act of god. By following the magnet's pull and reaching into each vessel. Making every man vassal. Every man author, and hero, to his own creation.

As he gets closer, the heat gets hotter, the more important it becomes that he be right. Because it seems easy. It becomes easy. As more and more of it makes sense. Until a man, who builds perfect things, must excuse his involvement in his own mistakes. This is hard. So he bleeds and screams to god.

To let go is a final act. In the face of what's coming that cannot be stopped. To forget to hold on is to submit to ride the flow exactly, regardless of the current's will or way. Or any of the wills swept by. Unless the flow itself can be altered. Unless men, with men for tentacles, can form a sort of weave and brace the medium which contains their consciousness.

Should he be able to find a common consciousness. Not one that creates any world where siren's songs are sung by dead martyrs. Who did the best they could while in such a daze. Nor a world colored wrongly in detail.

To grab full hold of the moment, he must find how we are as cells in a body.

21. Cells in a body. J's very clearly barely just holding on. His fingernails are bleeding and that makes him a threat to everyone around him. Some wounds must be bled to get the poison out. So he bears it. A long time ago, the parts of J that loved *him* bound the two of them in consequence. So that this wicked will could never wreak, what it wanted to, on one without wrecking the other. Because the parts of J that loved *him* knew that he had it in him. Those best parts of him that sat right beside the avenging will which, without a god to blame, would become the devil that summons him.

So J cast a spell to prevent a horror, in which he said the name of the horror aloud and accidentally invoked it. An enchantment, spoken in contrasts, intended to nullify what was only a possibility, which backfired. So an evil was born of it and remains to be dealt with.

There's no path upon which a man is not alone to deal with what he encounters. Though sometimes there are two or more wills involved when a man must deal with what he's done.

So J's alone with it, searching for the reflection of his saboteur in this horror he incanted. Since he's clearly unable to look at it directly. No matter. The faster the telling of this story is ended, the better. It's the story of a mistake that had to be made and its price. So that a boy, compelled toward what scares him, could be shocked to the core. So he could find and then refind it.

This is now every effort to lay a dead thing down in its grave. So all the new rules can finally apply and a new story can begin. J can say it over and over, refine and recant it, but, as long as he's saying it, part of his life is lost to the spell. This beautiful boy he imagined and the plagues of their misfortune. All their explanations and justifications and the lessons he needed them to learn.

He only needs to bide enough time to say it properly and have it said. Reword and dispel what's already dead to the author who's conceived of the end of it. Who wears an amulet, forged of all the elements plus two more, to protect against the worst of it. While the world around betrays, still, and the world within decays. For just a little while longer.

The conjuring's almost over and the conjuror soon will rest. J will wrap himself in his tendrils so he can amplify and cocoon. Feel only his own depravity until his attention burns it away. Then he can heal, begin to pupate and metamorphose. Until then, this is for everybody else. Even when he's finally a floating naked tumbleweed in the nexus of all infinities, J will still have always been Bodhisattva. And, what he did, he did this for them.

There are as many people around him as there are cells within. Plus that one thing in his blood, if he could only filter. This very real specter that haunts him. That one man walking around downtown who hasn't cut his hair in months. That one thing in J's blood, if he could only filter, that would make him so much stronger to be without.

The more desperate it becomes, the surer it be abolished, the more it seems to ooze, this sticky thing that won't let go. That one thing in J's blood that makes him weak from constant battle. Why a hug from a drunk friend's mother on her birthday makes him tremble. He's so sensitive now with all these tendrils, flailing. With all those people for suctioncups, feeling. Each of them bringing to him the state of their disease so he can dispel it to. Take it from them on some level, no matter what he'd rather, because everyone knows now, whether they know it or not, how easily he's infected.

It's incidental to that sort of connection, vibrating, that it travels both ways in time, revealing. How important it's become that he learns to channel. You can look into some people and know that their misery is infinite. Other people have just been crying and the depth in their eyes will wipe away for whatever the world demanded their water. They'll become more solid for the sake of it and stop reneging. The trade was the infinite for the moment. The sooner a man can understand this, and force out these impossible infinities that he cannot conduct, the more real he'll become for having navigated the meantime. The more he'll be able to navigate it better the next time around.

He's simpler for having orchestrated the million little wills which comprise him. Conducted their arrangement, in some fantastic way, to make his organism utensile. For consciousness or something like it to tool. Toil again for the sake of what's unavoidable and the chance to see beyond men's cycles as they stand on a spinning planet which stretches the paths they walk into spirals as it whizzes around a sun, around a galaxy, through a universe bound fractally, by the spiral, to naught. All of which serves only to raise a cacophony of white static swirling sine waves of each man's path begun perfectly just cells apart.

It'll take the singular will of a connected mankind to change the frenzy into the kind of resonant humming that will cleanse meaningless considerations from the minds of the many when they find singular reason to be. A basetone from which to consider the medium that carries the sound which men have just begun to hear. The harmony just underneath, or off in the distance, hinting about some order they can only just suspect. A song they think sung to them, drawing them to the source, by those siren men already humming pure tones.

It begins and ends with man, both ways in time. As a million cells comprise a millionth of all mankind. Contending with what comes in between. When a naked singularity is forsaken for the sake of what a shroud of experience obscures. And all the ways it's so easy to forget what holds them together. As impurities dilute the original identity in a million different hands, a million different ways, until the reason for it gets forgotten and must be refound.

Forgotten by all except the original will, whose faces watch from treetops and cloudforms. A piece of which is sewn into each man. For him to someday realize that some combination of circumstance and chance has wanted him into being. Maybe even wants a man, with too much on his mind, to learn to control his tool. Learn quickly enough that each piece implies the whole so that he can refuse whatever about the moment remains imperfect.

It might take the full sacrifice of his body and the full directed will of his mind to put him in a place where he can begin to live that sort of life. Despite each of their desires and what might pass between them. There's a version of this moment in which a man might surrender but that moment can only come after solid proof of the hand of god and all his sins forgiven.

First he must stand to face whatever problem his life has posed to jar him from his life. Stand brave against the sense of these new sensitivities and realize that what dies in his eyes, the other way in time, is born there. He must learn to repurpose and to channel the aspects of the universe that come to him. Ride waves of reason and consequence back past the end, full circle to his meantime, to know which step to take next.

J can no longer defend against any will who'd attack him, whether man or something baser or wilder. His body has stopped fighting. So, so must he. He sought the surest death and has no choice now but to refuse to acknowledge any sort of war. His only hope is to find an irresistible harmony and to hum it tsunamic. To wipe the face of the earth with its scourge, leaving only simple men, strong enough to manage what flows. Men who can believe the sun to be the center of the universe. Who can rewind what's been done and make everything else spin around a more familiar pivot.

Life is about to get dramatically different, by not changing at all. No matter. Just, the faces in the treetops and cloudtips will appear, as clearly, in those things floating around in your eye. Suddenly, you'll want to race to find a mirror and some men, not all of them, will note when you rush by. They'll recognize, in your gait and carriage, what used to take orchestras and amphitheatres, or mosaics in sanctuaries, to make clear. The art of being men with recognizable souls.

More than just the perfect story told by an image perfectly captured or a phrase phrased just right. Rather, the culmination of a man's refinement. Think of it. What might become of a man with all the nonsense out of the way, by the true sight of the daylight instructed. After all his pain's been made a soft lullaby to all those parts of him who'd hurt. All those stories he's been told about what's been done to him. Because he can finally feel that it's not real and he knows that there's no way to prove what really is. So it can't matter.

Instead, each man must clutch at common ground. He must fall to his knees, or be forced to fall, and pray to the dirt as he claws at it. Trying to scratch himself free of the hold of the ground underfoot. Until he exhausts himself and has no choice but to rest his tired body against it to sleep. So he might recognize his true importance in the answers given to him in small dreams. When what goes on, goes on without his consent or his involvement, and still changes him.

As he fulfills his role, like an ion in a bloodstream, sustaining certain truths and rushing to purge certain others. As some cells in his body are aligned to his purpose while some are maligned to different ends. Like some people, above a churning metal core, on a planet spinning around a thousand miles an hour, sixty-five thousand miles an hour around the sun, looking for each other. Lost below flocks of migrating birds and biplanes. Within a field but lost to it. Living just slightly misattuned to the sound that everyone's singing.

Guided by hints of needs and soft moments when it gets too hard. Soft embraces, in secret places, and the promise of things too soft to protect. Things that crumble. To remind him of his own innocence and what he's willingly forgone to reach beyond his separateness. Back to what the pull of the earth, and their spin around their star, suggests.

J knows that somewhere in the world is a man who can destroy him. If the man who failed to destroy him is any indication, who shattered himself, ramming, and remains only shards. Somewhere in the world is his equal, calling. A man, made in his image, across a glassy plane, whose threat of annihilation is the promise of peace.

Is the promise that the full force of the will to be, or not, will be made known to him an instant before they meet. In his eyes and what he recognizes that he can't possibly know. That soothes him more than it should. Not even a bother. Not even a question. Nothing left to struggle against once he's begun to feel the gathering pull of what promises to drag him, regardless, and land him square in front of an impossible fusion again. Like the mangled aborted one he'd already found, within a ten-year curse that wrecked him, only better.

Which is why he won't refuse it when it comes. Instead, he'll let the notion crash them together, as violently and magnetic as anything irresistible, and he'll use the momentum to stop time and those impossible worlds spinning around them. To become the center of an undesignated existence and to begin to build, to the best of their amplified might, a world intent on being.

For this, J decides to prepare himself. To design himself for this moment in order to summon it. By refusing to keep, from healing, wounds that would heal over if only left alone. By accepting the sum of all truths and by taking an inventory of man.

22. An inventory of man. His name's finally J. He will respond to that now without having to think about it. The same can be said for any of his nurtured psychoses, all comfortably themselves under a sky whose consensus is blue. Since blue's the only color left after the rest have been scattered. While interference patterns create buildings for men to wander safely between the worlds of each other. Into and out of what passes for days on the daylight side of men's dreams when no harmonic exists to be found.

This is the reason for the very real sense of sadness between men. Shaped into walls and cages, wherein certain men are allowed to affect certain others. Men build solid things to channel flows. Men have both poles of magnets inside them and they're made quickly aware of how such a force governs. It's a thing strengthened by proximity and possibility that can either bind or repel. Either way, it takes a very substantial dogma to defend against being affected, to remain impervious to another man's conduit. Enough to keep his soul's will from spilling over, if it happens that one man's not man enough to satisfy its aim. Until that one man is finally enough to conceive of what more than one man might do.

J walks around downtown Montreal having conversations with people in his head. He fishes into one lady's mind on the subway. She has glasses that are too big and her hair's inconspicuously cut. Not quite remarkably, she sits comfortably in an understated purple suit. With that smile, underneath, that she's trying to hide. Or to make common so that no one else suspects. J wonders why and says hi. She's surprised to hear him and reacts as though he's caught her in the nude. As though she's spent her days running a fingertip along the world and thinks that she's the only one. She stiffens in her seat, gets tense of brow and lip, and demands that he make sense. He asks her if she can feel it coming and she gets off at the next stop.

The more sensitive a man is to the heaviness, the more subject he is to the light. All men spend their lives discovering this, passing through the fields of other people. The more information a man gathers as he passes, the more appeal he holds for those creatures who fit into him. Who would try on, for a time, the prices of these most beautiful moments.

Some men are obviously able to bear more than others. The allure of this promise nearly always summons consequence. Which is why it might take the best of a man's potential to conjure the worst of what he wreaks. If that's how his tool is sharpened, dragged across the stones at whatever pace a man might walk the path of his life.

Because J could not bear the other man's infinite pain, now he has to. He's an idealist, above all else, and refuses to stop believing until the best has finally come. Now he has to understand if he wants to remain unaffected or be forced to watch it all be undone. His heart will beat black blood if it has to. It doesn't matter so long as it flows. In this sense, no man's life is his own. The path that he follows can only be seen from above. He who walks it must remain a man of faith, impenetrably pious, if he's to conduct his own very real moments in between insanities. Those flashes of a very real romance, in between slaps that blacken, in which they laugh and bells ring when they kiss. In which they pretend to speak German and fall asleep holding each other all night long, witnessing miracles together while that thing, that's eating him, gets bigger.

What hurts J most is that he can't love him anymore, whose name he won't say lest the image hear its name. Not that he can't love anymore because he can love and has loved since. What hurts is that he can't love *him* anymore. This cork and the pressure building. What hurts most is that J's jealous of anything *he'll* ever love. Anything J can barely see through the tinted green glass of his bottle. Mostly those tinted things that he loves about himself. Being him, J imagines, as he waits for someone else to love again. Being in love is a glamour, a being in love, created by genies in bottles.

J's capable of the idea that a man's soul and his animal are two separate things, and that love is made of light which is of the soul. But he's not capable of the idea that a man might love himself. There's still the duality to heed. The trinity in the states of man, either no or yes, if yes, either negative or not, to account for the prices of things. There's some trapdoor, best kept latched, in which a hole is defined by something other than the edges that surround it. Which is a thought best suited for a desert mountaintop and not one he'll address here. He's not brilliant enough yet to talk about the entire universe as just the edge of a hole. Give him time.

So back to it. J knows that no one will laugh with the other man the way that J did. He's disappearing while J flails to find some way to believe that they had something special. So he can move on. This is what it takes to end his animal's lament. Its long howl at the moon, trying to convince itself that there's no other love like that for him. That it was him who failed it, not J. Surely not J. It was J's perfect love to inspire and to swell full with. The other's flailing and he's disappearing and he's being punished by god. J hates the monster that swallowed the man that he still loves and can't get to. Whoever it is who originally blasphemed. Who turned god against both of them and sent them, one at a time, away from the rapture.

It wasn't J's first instinct to turn from god. He didn't think it was possible in the light of his intentions. So when the time came, and the time always comes, he was unprepared and had to do what felt right. What he was able to sense at that moment, in the sense that a holy choice needed to be made through a not-forgotten son who forsook a brighter light for one not so far away. Which sounds like such a romantic deed, if he didn't need his exile in order to feel and to wield the full force of his torment in order to make, of it, great things.

J's found a way to draw power from never again because he had no source to draw from after everything had gone away. Nothing but a book of blank pages upon which he's seen and found these truths and other things in the patterns of the overlapping ripplings of men's minds. Truths about entireties and the directions they tend. From that deep black longing which is all the deeper for that single speck of light, shimmering like the one from which he's been banned. He'll get as close as he can bear, without fear now of ascending, or fear of slipping back, just to feel the source with physical hands, as close as skin to skin, then deeper. To finally be able to withstand awe and to go knowingly about its bidding. He'll use these truths, like a superconductor magnet, to call out another star, then to dilate. With his growing sense of what he can do.

It's this realization that severs the last of the twitching nerves between them, leaving none left that might spasm. No matter. These two are still as surely bound as always. They'll always have nerves between them but, now, only phantom ones that hum.

Like a surgeon closing. After hacking through skin and muscles, to get near bone, to fix a bleeding thing. Then fixing it. Then stepping backwards out, sewing muscles to reconfigure form to serve purpose. Sewing a scar into a face, using words as sutures. This is what J's been doing. Solving love, solving longing. Invoking the power of lingual gods to dispel the last of a lingering curse. Sometimes words are like homing pigeons trained to one of your eyelashes. Sometimes like ravens with dead snakes clasped tightly in their claws.

A man must sever himself from his past. Drop whatever he's been dragging and stand his ground. He must become industrious man and go about his life in strange ways, tapping on its glass with a knife. Trying to carve hieroglyphs into diamonds.

J sees something glisten. His attention catches something perfectly poetic in the idea of something that cannot be marked. The thought of this lets loose a hundred tentacles, once planted in all those horrible memories, like roots, like the nine hundred other tentacles still feeding on that rot. Rot feeds life and life feeds rot. Though life feeds life as well. It's really just a matter of choice.

J decides to plant himself on a shoreline that he must wander through life to find. A thousand steps away from where he is no longer and who's no longer there beside him. The wind folds waves up over his feet and slowly sucks him down. His tendrils reach back along the breeze for someone in possession of what he's looking for. What he'll only recognize upon suffering his reaction to it. Two steps behind the tide rising around the jaw of a planted man who mistook the seafloor for fertile ground. No matter. He's holding his breath either way to sharpen his senses by listening more closely.

The world hasn't been the same for J ever since that impossible word, lithium, was picked from his brain by a boy who's still not smart enough to choose himself sane. Since then, J's known more about reality than his animal permits. Nor will he say. He's afraid that they're watching so he only goes as far as it takes to find an edge. He doesn't push. He just notes it and uses it to define his sense of how big it might be and where he must run should the time come. His own ignorance has become a cue and call to suspicion. In this sense, he's been refined as he goes about mapping the invisible contours of a labyrinth on a piece of paper he keeps folded up in his shoe.

It happened when they were driving back from a long trip they took to get away from the place they were returning to. The place that made one of them mad. It was J's idea to show him the mountains. He'd never seen the mountains. This is when J had no choice but to make it real, after seeing something other than a man, in the shape of a man he knew, on the shores of Lake Superior, foaming from the mouth, screaming and ranting impossible thing. Even after he'd seen the mountains. Still somehow unaware of how the earth heals. This is when J was forced to realize, to wonder to himself what drug they give to obvious schizophrenics. Which is when he had the impossible word "lithium" picked from his brain. Since then, J only questions answers he's gathered and he doesn't ever speak about the faces in the woods.

J's also being punished by god. According to what one of his family members once said of men like him and the prices they pay for loving each other, without a god's consent. This is why J hasn't said a word to anyone. Why he's spent his time better trying to orient his field, to say its name to destroy the monster that ate his lover. The one he still looks for everywhere and hopes to never see.

He must either be able to master the flow or become able to stand against it. Which is really no choice at all if any word of this manifesto is to be taken seriously. He must align himself to signs, to flows and harmonies, and the chance to see the world turn red. He doesn't fear that anymore. Neither the signs, nor the harmony, nor the tide of the light when its weave begins to unravel. He's absently managed the incarnation once already, both ways in time. He counts this as another in his inventory and sees that the balance is nearly maintained. It remains now only to test it.

The thought of finally knowing peace plays on his strings like a symphony. A song whose playing numbs his senses with an excitement that's too fast and perfect. It feels like anxiety. Which is really just an inundation. An influx of too much information to be sorted.

There are two ways to calm a racing heart: The heart itself can be slowed by changing its reason for beating or time can be slowed with respect to a man's awareness of it. So a man might react quickly enough to brace himself against the hammer of each fibrillation and surf each pulse for the thrill of it. Go completely fucking crazy. So he can watch which parts quiver when he lets loose and gets dragged into the heart of his beast. To take on the full form of his dragon to see if he can bear what it sees and all those other senses. And, if he can't bear it, then to finally be sure what's left. What's more than just water and meat. If anything.

He's seen realities unlike any other. He's seen that the same can be said of anyone out here, any perception or perceiver. That every man is out here alone, his way defined by each step he takes to walk it, no two of them headed the same way, exploding from a common point, falling.

23. Completely fucking crazy. It's all spinning, tracing corkscrews through the night. The earth round the sun, round itself, hurled through the darkness. One man's body, on the spinning earth, is sad. So he learns, when it wakes him with nightmarish chemicals that bleed into his days. J spends his time drawing inhabitable faces in his little black book, searching for expressions. Any sign of some otherworldly empathy to which he might cling. As the pains of this world flood past regardless, dragging him along. As he claws at dry trees on mountaintops.

Every day, for a thousand years, a crack in a white stone mountain has yawned with each pass of the sun. Its beat counts out time, sends out vibrations through what listens. Its rhythm is the harbinger of life. One day, one flap of a butterfly's wing swats the sound through time. It ripples around the planet for another thousand years before a series of convergences amount to a whisper, on a twirling wind, in an alleyway, that only a man, with a sad body, is in the right place to hear. It whispers, "I love you too," to a man who's said, "I love you," so many times before.

Within those thousand years, as that message waited for that man, a sapling sprouted. It grew from a crack in a white stone mountain, having heard the call of the beat of the sun for years. It stretched through the yawning crack to reach for what called to it, the source of some pattern to feed on. It takes only one fact for something like a crystal to grow, for it to hum, like a rock thrown into water. Suffering whatever it takes to get there.

The seasons cycle suns. The rains come winter snows. The tree grows to the metronome of these machinations. Its roots reach deeper into the crack in the rock when it swells in the heat of the day. Holding ground while it reaches for heaven. Motivated by the arrangement of its matter, its need to cycle through its own consequences of being, devouring light to rearrange itself, to take inventory of purpose and necessity and to extend.

A word can define the edge of a thing, like *hole* or *god*, or it can be a thing's name. Just as the source of any creature's motivation is what defines him. It's his strongest reference point and all his reason. If properly aimed, it will get him within range of his goal and the satisfaction of his purpose. To know a man's motivation is to know the path of his life and to which truth his will adheres. Every other rule, along the way, is negotiable. His life is like a balloon on a string. The lives of men connect like balloon strings, floating off in all directions, tugging at a little boy's hand.

Which is why a tree, growing in a crack on a white stone mountain, is unmoved when a man, with very strong human emotions, climbs the mountain to sit next to it. The tree is more aware of the overlapping of their fields than the man is while he's distracted by clumsier senses.

Despite his sad body, J's happy in all directions. In his most brilliant days, every step he takes is deliberate. This day, a climb to the sun has led him to a tree on a mountaintop where he sits and pours a nubile sense of life across the countryside as they share a sun. Both high enough to have a common sense of an oncoming storm.

The path of a storm can be known by the shape of the clouds if a man's seen the clouds before and has paid attention. Every so often a man is just fucking beautiful after climbing a mountain or noticing the lives of men disappearing. Whatever it takes to get there. It's then that he looks up and sees the faces of past lovers and expressions from unlived lives watching him from patterns in treetops.

J asks himself which sense he used to know these things, to recognize such songs on breezes, realizing that a sad boy tends to see what's familiar. He hopes that he's finally walked far enough to let it be. To step fully in or to step fully out. To keep from further disturbing the water.

To get back to himself, after walking the full distance to another, a man must turn his back. Trust that he's on his own, in decision and consequence, enough to spot the devil in his fear. A man should never mistake the devil that he keeps for a pet. The devil he feeds doesn't serve him. It's tricked him so that it can eat. Devils eat what festers and rots. To finally rid himself of all his devils forever a man must counter their wills by eating only life.

Life must be hunted. It's prey. It hides from men, frightened by men's tendency to defile. In the sense that "to enlighten" means "to make into light" and any enlightened man with eyes is a cannibal. Man's a ruminant whose second stomach is vestigial. He exists in a low energy state of indigestion. Man lacks in his ability to be nourished. He's been uprooted and must conclude his satisfaction. He has a nervous disorder, pertaining only to his brain, that evolution has casually reflected.

That's what it took to get here. Men's minds cycling through baptismal moments to find themselves anew, hoping soon to be ready to find another, heeding the magnet's draw despite the folded cloth between them. Coming closer and closer to actual meaning. Everyone sees the meaning in J's words but they don't always know quite what it is. He sees this as the distance between them. Two sets of skin and the speed of light.

J once met a man from Babylon who told him a creation myth. J was lost, somewhere, wandering through the desert. He'd run away from familiar things to where strange things couldn't say his name and he could call himself whatever he willed. Lost deep to the sways of what he trusted as whims. Though the sun had risen and set more times than he'd seen, as many times as it takes to get a man to a mountaintop, before a storm, where a sapling's become a tree.

The man from Babylon, as J helped him on his way back home, told J that the devil is depicted with no hands in stone carvings on the walls of ancient Babylonian ruins. The Babylonians believed that man existed as only an idea in the mind of god before any man had ever walked the earth or been taught anything of loneliness by love.

Time began when god considered what might be implied by his own existence, a question of the opposite of omniscience. It's from this idea that man was born, a single thing, certain only of his self, contained and unable to ever grow enough, no matter how much he was fed. An ego singularity was such a beautiful notion to an omnipotent creature. The beauty of something able to suffer what it might take to get there.

It was this curious god's consideration of opposites that created room for the devil, as well. And faces where there shouldn't be faces at all. The devil, to the Babylonians, is sometimes represented as god's shadow though this metaphor is only meant to be seen by high priests, steeped in context, in the deepest crypts, lest the idea confound. The devil was born by contrast, of the same stuff as man but always more. Man is not god in every sense while the devil is only not god in one.

The idea of the devil is an accident, born of god's unrestrainable will, incidental to thoughts of opposites. Simultaneously equal and inferior. The devil is all the things that god is not. Thereby he exists beyond god's concern and the whole that the two might fill.

It outraged the devil to be a creature of equal might and breadth as god but born of the same stuff as man. He was born, he'd been given time, and next to his god he would always be a tantruming child. So he watched as god toyed with his new notion and remained unconcerned with him. The devil knew shame that god was more interested in the play of push and roll than him, of consequences and the suffering of them. When really it was the notion of ignorance god worshipped.

The devil grew jealous and angry, subject to time now and waiting. He was forced to put all his infinite nature into understanding separate and alone while god was infinitely focused on a finite riddle, stuffing all his infinite glory into as many men as he could imagine and playing out all the combinations of their lives. While the devil waited to feel that sort of thing. To feel what it might be like to be subject to god's fascination.

Until he'd been kept separate for too many eternities, too long, for the sake of those small things, which were separate, like him, but not alone. Until the devil grew too jealous and angry and his jealousy and anger turned to rage. He gathered each man from god's mind, reached into the mind of god and clasped his hands around each man in turn. He plucked them from god to hold them separate, from each other, and from god. Which is why the devil's drawn with no hands. The bones of his hands became the cage of each man's ribs when the devil made manifest what god was only thinking.

To the Babylonians, man was born of betrayal and revenge, pulled jealously from the mind of an autistic god, as god remained contentedly in his heaven, aware of the devil's schemes only by their reflection in the beating of men's hearts. Until god sees through all-time what comes of men's longing. Until he doesn't understand it and loses interest. This horrible longing that casts spells in men's world to conjure mythologies beyond a disinterested god. To leave god to the obsolete while men go about making religion from the matters at hand.

As J sits, attending the storm, by the tree in a crack in a white stone mountain, he considers this notion of man, conceived of god and born of the devil, made of the same stuff as both. He sees that god is insane. He sees that it doesn't matter. Thoughts about the devil and god raise questions of morality, irrelevant to the order of men. It's too important that J holds his place. Besides, there's only one thing left that he'll willingly learn through contrast. One thing he'll spend as much time as it takes to find, do whatever it takes to get. That god, to his devil, who'll hold him so he can finally let go and become the full conduit to god's will across realities. Bodhisattva brings each man back to god so he might bow and make his choice.

On his way to the mountain, on the back of a washroom stall, J writes, "on the other side of this door is every choice you will ever make." When he writes the same thought in his little black book, as he eats his lunch on a nearby shore, a seagull laughs at him. So he shares his lunch with it. It eats half his sandwich and gets so excited by the taste of a cookie that it flies to the middle of the lake and loses it to the water. Not so funny anymore though J laughs, unsure what he's supposed to conclude. He sees porcupines cross the road when he absently thinks things he should note: The fox that finally died. This is no different.

The faces in the storm usher him to move faster. J races to stay ahead of it. When he reaches the mountain the storm's still far off. He has time to savor the daylight as he hikes away from the roads and the trails left by men. He fools himself that he might wander where no man has stepped before but he doesn't believe it. He knows that he'd have to stand upon a wave tip somewhere in the middle of the ocean to be free of the residue men leave. He's followed his body's will to places where it seemed there was no hum of man only to find paintings on cave walls. He's followed it to where crystal caverns have gathered men's humming and raised it to another harmonic. This is no different.

So he sits by a tree growing in a crack in a white stone mountain and waits for the rain to come. He closes his eyes, satisfied by what he's done to get here. He finally feels peace after having forged the story of a good man from the details of his life. And uncovered a path that a good man might walk to nirvana. He knows it will lead him to the water's edge before the time comes for him to stop walking.

Before he's able to think any thought a single moment further, his hairs raise suddenly as a crack of lightning splits the tree beside him. It's deafening and the gesture of the tree's limb falling summons a quick dense rain. The static in the air stands his tentacles on end. He should be afraid but for some reason the smell of smoke soothes him. He's chosen the ending already and walks too bravely through a world that's ended him once before. No matter. He's stepped fully into the moment by now and has reason to believe the things he senses, having run far enough away from the screaming to finally be able to hear. By listening closely.

Men's awareness is spread like a net across the globe. His science and technology are intended to build more and more bridges that span greater and greater distances to the point where two men's minds, on either side of the world, can be linked directly. It's the evolving nature of the culture of men. They crave the mind of god again. To know his role as defined by the place he holds in the field of all men around him. The same way a cell in a tree knows which function to serve based on a sense of its place amongst kin. So it grows, subject to how much of the sun's light's filtered, how much water can be drawn up, what the cells nearby are charged to do and why, through time and the cycles of all these things. It's the instinct of the god construct.

It grows toward some greater end for reasons sprung up all around it. What it can do, defined by where it sits, how it got there and the consequences of both these things. Some purpose contrived from the harnessing of circumstance and proximity used to consider the simple unfolding of solid things falling. This meantime might be the only time but that doesn't mean that what follows can't be affected.

The pull of the planet underneath these creatures, who cling to its face as it whizzes through space, trains the direction and the reach of things that grow. Unless, like men and their machines, they grow cancerously and can only hope for spontaneous evolutions in the form of mutations or whatever else might lead to conclusions and to things transcending. Which is why J walks toward a tree, growing in a crack in the white stone mountain, during a lightning storm.

The rain pours down as though the sky's become an ocean and has begun to fall. The lightning from the sky, calls smoke from the torn tree, becomes steam as its embers sizzle. It's the clap of significance that marks the convergence of choice and circumstance. Having rippled both ways in time to summon a tree from the ground centuries before it spurred a man onto his journey. From overhead, having judged which man's path might be swayed sufficiently, by the addition of a snowflake to a blizzard or an extra sparkle to a wave tip that's not the reflected sun, which is all the ballrolling an otherworldly will might muster. Which, in some cases, is more than enough.

And none of it's any more absurd than all the rains and snows of the cycling seasons, all the insects gnawing and the acid rain, all the sunless days and moonless nights, altering the nature of a growing thing. Incorporating into its structure and form, and ultimately its purpose, something that might resemble a man's face looking back, should a crack of lightning tear it free. So that the first thing it sees, when the smoke clears and the world's finally revealed, is J waiting to greet it.

24. Men's lives disappearing. It's not the easiest thing to spot. But the lives of men are disappearing. Long before the men themselves disappear. They're being erased from the experience of others. A trade of momentum just rips them out when they finally see clearly enough to reach in and grab it. Which is only true in estimates and opposites. It's more likely that these men simply start to spin and then stop. Spin for the sake of the sun so it can rest for a moment. For the sake of the planet, for the same reason. For everyone in the meantime relative to everyone else. Then they stop. They become a godpoint around which the rest of it pivots.

It's half as easy as finding an existing god or letting go entirely. It's finally understanding the warmth of the light against a man's skin. From within the closest star, to beyond the farthest, and all the images in between. It's taking sense from a man's place in the world, without interpretation, to know what's really going on. Standing in the heat of it. Seeing some reality take shape in the flames without mistaking the faces in the fire for tricks of the light. Wisely preferring trickless realities.

Watching, instead, which stuff tends which things. Hoping to glimpse the deepest truth he might. Past heartache, past longing, past god even. A man, searching for god, quickly realizes that he needn't take a single step. Part of the godsong, he aches to hear, speaks about how he'd be better off closing his eyes and humming. It's the easiest thing in the world to remember god. All a man needs to do is clarify his ignorance. Then he must quickly brace himself because it's going to flail. He needs to be prepared to watch a thing die. Especially if bad things have been done to him. Because it's dying right there next to him in the cage they share. And whatever unanswered questions might leave a man drawn to the death throes of things are about to be answered.

No matter how good it's felt before, or how bad it feels now, he must resist the urge to look away. He must find some strength to draw upon so he can stand against what urges plague him. The urge to help, which is usually just a grotesque expression of empathy, or the urge to put a flailing thing out of its misery. He must be enough to realize that he's able to feel, that he cannot be made to feel, and that he's here for only that reason. The sensations themselves must remain irrelevant beyond the moment. What they ask of him is total subjugation. He must remain solid while caught in the flow. He must remain gathered or bleed away. He must be sure the thing is dead and that it's finally over.

Once consequence is summoned it demands its price. When time is set into motion, for a man to grow, he must consume. A man must grow or else he withers. So a man must consume in order to be a man. He must decide, then act, then consume. This must be the way of things until he finds a more abundant source he might rest by. It's built into every cell in his body as it's built into every man in mankind. A compulsion to be voracious that he wakes to one day. Suddenly, he's enthralled, amazed to find that there are things he must do. As well, there are things he will feel. He's the last pillar standing in the river of time passing by.

Time is jealous and vengeful and meticulous. Eroding the weary with consequences and willing other things undone. She is the space between infinities. Her patterns are random eddies, in impossible places, where opposing truths cannot be reconciled so they become men. She's the nature of enduring, having watched the awareness of sentient men subdivide one moment like a zygote forming. She's infected by them. They share a space that both must endure.

A man must endure. He must believe that things always change for the better. He must make it that way. Though, at times, he'll be of too many perspectives and too hard to convince. His body's being hacked away at. Losing more of the ability to resist infestation every day. Affected by the ripples, rewriting lives in both directions. Unable to resist the will of the influx to change him. Unable to aim, through consequence, sharply enough to keep the variables from changing what his efforts intend. So it mustn't matter.

He can no longer rely on outcome for sustenance. He must wield in ribbons if he's to brace himself or to have any impact at all. Should he will it. He must flow broader and reach for the ribbons of those floating around him. To begin the weave between infinities. To brace the moment, in its final throes, and to hold it when it's gone. The time has come when he must find some way to accept how it unfolds and to sit. He must figure himself amidst the flows before he can become fully one thing or the other. He must find his way to some fascinating place, stand there, then step out of the way. If he's to become occupiable, enough to make the decision, he must prove that he can be trusted.

He must watch his own death throes. He has to know which parts are his and which parts are not, which parts which will sustains and which parts are better off dead. If he's ever to be whole, he's to watch the parts of himself that other people carry around with them too. All the parts he's given away as well as all the ones they've just taken. He must watch, as the lives of men disappear and either scavenge his parts back when they fall or grow to encompass the world. Regardless, the utmost truth he must embrace is that none of this will be over until he lets it. The rest he must simply endure.

This is the solution. For a man who's been made too scared to move. Who slept outside the train station, who took that man into his home. A man humbled by a god who refused to entertain him for the sake of the path he's walked regardless of what the unfolding of time did to him. Whether it left him alone in this world or not, made more real than anyone else he knows, eclipsing the god above from the awareness of the devil below. A parting of infinities, splitting like a fertilized egg. While, around him, he's the last man alive as the rest keep disappearing. He's the harbinger of this, the shepherd oracle staking his staff to fork the trail, offering each man his holy choice by saying it out loud. That it's his fault. He's capable of the will to manifest. And the time has come for one man. So the time's come for them all.

It's the war of solid versus light, with every tactic decided by loyal foot soldiers, in the thick of it, who've been cut off from command and have only their faith in the sense of their cause as guiding morality. Obscured somewhere within a sense of their connectedness and the weariness that accompanies it. As each man tries to rally the rest to reach what one man alone cannot touch. At least not without a certain idea of the pattern of his image in the deluge. Unless he's sure of where to look to find faces in the static. As light through yonder window breaks. He must understand enough to keep tactile while managing to conduct the sublime. Lest the deluge tear him open, unravel his half-truth and take, from him, his ability to choose.

There's no line to be drawn between a man and his holiness. There's only the matter of his consent. Which makes it possible that all of mankind might spontaneously transform. This is the age of man's death throes and not all men will survive. It's about to get very hard but any man, who's truly searching for himself, can get used to anything. His full certainty of his involvement in his life makes him formidable. Even if he mistakes shards of glass for crystal sculptures. Or is fool enough to believe in faery tales, from faraway lands, whose physics he can't possibly understand. He has the right to his moment once he's asked the question and has said "yes" to it.

He simply must witness and endure. A man standing atop the only thing can only jump up. If he chooses to jump at all. It's the same thing whichever way he's facing and it's all just what hydrogen does. That's not what's going on here. That's what it took to get here. The patterns of a man's life can be traced on paper to see the sigil they form. It can then be charged by the act of full abandonment of self and the curse cleared by penance so that one man might conclude a cure for his disease and infect the rest of the world with it. To quiet the screaming voices which cacophony as they fall, rippling chaotic into being through the opposite of the opposite of that.

First, he'll need to get to a safe place or create room for the idea of a safe place to get to. He must take only drugs that stimulate and be capable of absolute trust, still, even if he's been betrayed every other time. He must turn his back and expose his soft underbelly, call upon all the consequences of one side to see what's left after Armageddon. It's time to clarify the idea of self. More than just the suffering of consequence, or cartography of the organism, a man's life is the possibility of sentient communion. It's time to commit to a perspective and to let the rest scatter on the wind. Or something like it. Because there's much to discuss.

It's to this thought that half of his tentacles disappear. In the same way that the two dimensions of a plane can be seen from above or below but, on its level, a man of more dimensions can see that it's just not there. Just as a country can hardly be described by its border. Or a path, by the lone man who walks it. Who can't know the experience of the path ahead of him and only subjectively remembers the path he's walked so far. Each exists as only hints and implications in the other's reality. So, too, does a man become aware that he might reach further if he can stretch in all the right ways to feel with other tools. So long as he can remain keenly aware of, and never confuse, all the ways in which he's falling.

So he can find those traits of his character that he might unfurl as wings. To glide or to hover like a damselfly braced on the winds. Some men carry themselves aware of their sticks and pivots, others aware of their stalk. For some, the ether's thickened, and he must grow tentacles or wings to move more gracefully through.

The way a man dances reveals what he knows of his matters, how he thinks and why he stumbles. Each man's awareness of his graces has to be refined before he can figure how to fly. After finding proof of god, a man must conclude theory and begin its application. Proof of god sets a chain of events into motion that a quick man will construe as proof of himself.

These are volatile days in which we find ourselves living. If we're actually looking and are actually alive. What each man accepts as truth has the power to fluctuate with the beat of a hummingbird's heart. A man need only be convinced of it. Which is why everyone who asks for a sign is getting one. As well as all of the consequences of asking. It has something to do with that new look, not quite there yet, in people's eyes. The one they sense or recognize and thoughtlessly crave to see through. Through all the old perspectives that are being nullified, with all the new ones coming in, and what sorts of power a man might catch from noting, while the world ends because there's no reason for it not to.

When the time comes, a man must've long sensed it coming if he's to be ready. So his animal won't be startled and bolt, knowing that what he's about to witness will be explosive. In one way or another, he must be made aware of the possibility of absolute catastrophe. If he's to stand objectively enough to observe what's real, knowing that the time will come when he'll have to choose. He can either scamper about searching for stronger footholds or become one of the siren men humming the end to crescendo. Finding safe harbor in the nodes between vibrations where pools of life are implied by the mathematics of each harmonic.

It's best that each man take the time to listen as soon as he feels it approach. He needs to be ready to watch a thing die to see what sort of peace it makes with its last moments. For insights into how to make his own. To catch power from it. Because the sensing of it is enough to bring it near. Possibility ripples the space between things like raindrops on the surface of a still ocean. Below the surface, the ripples grow like halved spheres, like stars at the very edge of the universe gone supernova. Each crest's a different expression on the same face of a Russian nesting doll. While men, in the air above, suddenly breathe deeper breaths for the taste of some subtle bliss they've held both halves of, just at different times.

Men spread the idea of this rapture infectiously. This one defined by contrasts through some gateway with a familiar keyhole. It's in every way any two of them might connect. A smile from across a lonely crowded room, an embrace in the moment it's needed, a rough sweaty fuck till you wake wrapped around him in the morning light. All the things a man suffers without, regardless. He suffers but cannot know why without knowing from what he's been severed. He must find a substantial faith and trust it to guide him through the unraveling light. The light is as near to unraveling as it's ever been. This can either be the opening of a gateway to his soul on the other side or it can be the cauterization of a wound. A knot tied in man's true umbilicus to stop the bleeding. To save both mother and child.

The last plague will be the plague that threatens to sever man from his soul. This is all that's left to suffer, the final death throes, tendrils of which men feel rippling through the meaning of their lives. Some men are already shivering, cut off from all sources of heat and light. They are example. Not really men at all. Other men have survived all sorts of infection and are aware enough of self to know where self begins and where, by implication, it might end. They've got holes in their feet full of fish eggs and larvae because they dared to jump. Not a word need be mentioned about the boys they've kissed. Especially not the one with that look in his eyes that was there once, and found worth loving, but not there the rest of the time. Or ever again. The one who went off alone to die behind a dumpster, like a wounded lonely alleycat, while greater men transcended and took everyone else with them. Learned the lessons of their lives and passed on their truths to amplify all of mankind.

25. The damselfly. J makes it to the water's edge. He's walked as long as it took to get here, dragging a ribbon behind him, draped across the path of his life. He's been made mad and sits to watch the damselfly for a moment before going on. He lets the reach of his other senses drift off beyond his concern. He's weary about all that's behind him, all that's pushed and followed him here, so he rests. Closes all those senses that are not his eyes and watches till he learns what it means to be another thing.

A man is three times removed when he remembers his dreams, recombined from things he's done and failed to do. He's twice removed when he lives his life, things he's not fully suffered and still must endure. Once, as he searches the world for what he's intended.

It's when a man aligns with his purpose that he draws their attention near. All the faces converge upon the moment when a man's greatness approaches. Ripples of it bounce from the shores of oceans all around him, out to and back overtop horizons. He'll see them more and more in treetops and cloudforms as he wanders. He's followed the swiftest river to the opposite of its source and now sits by the water's edge before going on, watching the life of a different thing for refuge.

J hesitates. He's tired after two full years of being followed by that indistinguishable man in the dark trenchcoat under the lamppost in the rain. Whether friend or something other, he's elusive, too comfortable in the shadows and alleyways to ever confront directly. J sees no other way through but to trust him. So he turns to expose his back. Which is what he must do to finally leave him behind.

He's different for what follows him. That is all. He must leave what lurks to the shadows and its consequenceless periphery so he can move on to more consequential things. He hopes for some sense of how to go on. It's been two years of the same lame cud and there's no more nourishment to be had from it. There's only chalk left in his mouth from the grinding of his teeth. And a crippling yearning to go on.

Which doesn't explain his hesitation. But does explain his ache. The yearning is crippling. His hesitation is his own inaction. There's no more sense there to be made than that. His body remembers too vividly what the rest of him would forget. Better remember with hieroglyphic incantations, not yet painted, on crystal walls in caves. On all the rigid walls built around the flows of what's his life. That he can only walk between, through loopholes and siphons, from cell to cell. His hesitation is his curiosity about the body these cells might comprise. The one that he bleeds through. By now, he's mapped the outside of the labyrinth and knows that there's no way out. So he sits.

In this reprieve of self, he finds it more interesting to observe the paths of two creatures coinciding, in front of him, in the air above still water. Their names don't matter. Not while serving their function, despite themselves. Some greater will sparks between them and, like tinder, they begin to burn. The white flames flicker like ideas, cycling curious faces who have come to mark the beginning to the path of something else's meantime.

The reflection of these creatures in the water contains expressions beyond their experience. Regardless of what they've seen or what sets of events their lives have set into motion, this moment of their full purpose is witnessed for the sake of what comes after they've gone. After they've followed the events of their unraveling lives and ended finally in a mindless embrace to recombine information from happenstance according to some greater design.

A million years of patterns of variables are reflected in the water below two entangled creatures, hovering. It takes two of them to make one will to go on. Rewarded by ecstasy in the serving of their purpose. Half of each is required, born of the fire between them, in the air, then dropped, through the water, to continue a single path beyond them. The later part of an eternity, spiraling in both directions, that only passes through them as they go about their days. Taking time from other pursuits to heed the call of their mechanism. Under the brightest midday sun, in a universe that's halves of itself, their barest nature commands their dance for the sake of the single falling sphere that comes of it. Dropped into the water.

It falls, as solid things do, drawn together by love or by gravity. Drawn to whatever might keep them from falling any further, whether by choice or subject to the will of other forces. It's the most primitive instinct: The first react. Of whatever creature, hatched of whatever egg, laid by whatever laid it. All the way back through generations of mutation, before life, back to where only patterns emulated. Back further, to the first instant, when the first atoms fell from the sun. To erase any notion that love is anything more than an instinct intrinsic to the physics of this sort of being. Between before and after.

The egg falls into one of the valleys of the washboard seafloor where the flow of salted water, spun for aeons around the solid world, has drafted the design of a man's ribcage. Which is the same as drafting the man himself. Regardless of prophecy or inevitability, the egg has only the memory of where its patterns have been, whether recorded or not, encoded in the arrangement of its matters or simply still humming, like a tuning fork, from a song it once heard. Living out the expected path of a thing falling into being. Subject to the whims of what matters.

From its own experience, it has only the sense of falling. How that's reflected in changes of pressure and shape while a life gathers from the fire, through the air, solidifying as it ages. Not yet reacting, just falling. Chasing the necessities of its construct until it stops, or is stopped, rests on the seafloor and learns to depend upon the calmer sense of being held. In its first moments, it becomes aware of time, of having fallen, and of place. The sensing of which implies before, and after, and elsewhere. And comfort from all these things.

While chemicals react as chemicals will. Chains of events inspire chains of events that might amount to a vessel that a life might fill. As the tides sweep up over craggy shorelines, smashing fragile things to make room for things that are stronger, luckier or more clever. That can hold their shape, through all the smashing, to house the patterns and their will to tangle. Drawn like a magnifying glass, by an old man, across names on a list. As though time itself is just what a man might make of the details of his condition.

Just the moment inflated by a man's awareness of what might transpire. What stories he's able to remember, enough to tell, that explain how the details ended up the way they did. Governed by all the senses and the sense he's able to make of them. To get him as far along the list as he can, ruling out name after name, searching for something bigger than his organism. The man who'll bring the matchstick to the man who built the pyre.

Searching for that fascinating combination of circumstances, scavenged from amongst all the wrongsized pieces, that he feels strongly enough to suspect might be his brilliance. Those subdivisions of character, brought to him by fellow wanderers who've been to other places and who've brought back shards that complete his arrangements. Like an egg just fertilized, suddenly dividing into a brain, capable of detail enough to capture the moment to grab hold, like infestation, and feed upon the life of it. Channeling the lengths and the depths of its ancestry and legacy to remain solidly himself. For the moments he'll feel compelled to witness with a perspective honed by the path. Until finally he coincides as the last shard needed to fuse what's cracked. To contain all the light that would bleed. He knows that all the light is needed to distract from certain darks.

If the vessel doesn't fuse then it can never be filled. It will bleed whatever light inhabits. A man can't, for long, stay distracted. He can't trust what stays broken after the last piece is in place. The scent of his hope will lure predators. As will remembering any sense he's already made. He should quickly move on unless for some reason he sees a need to hide there for just a moment longer.

Whether it be loose threads to an unconvincing plot or the suspicion of a greater combination of words. He must muster confidence in what he's done. If he's to generate euphoria, he must build upon contentedness. Which means that he must let it be. Let a wound become a scar. He's begun his life's work but other lives keep interfering. He's growing anxious. He knows, from experience, that a distracted man will be made violently aware when his attention is needed, regardless of his other intentions. His resistance is a conflict of wills as is every difficulty of his life.

So J takes his time. He sees that the egg, on the seafloor, has become another creature. It split in half, a million times, to become a single thing. A complicated little collection of clever instructions have unfolded, have made order out of need, and function, by dividing. He sees that empathy has connected the minds of each of these small cells with their commonness of situation and purpose. From this awareness has beat an organ. It pumps a will of cycling waters to sustain the arrangement that makes it, serving a singular purpose perpendicular to what its choices and inclinations might do. To build a single mechanism that will be called upon to serve this purpose while it goes about living its life, both ways in time and direction.

J slides the magnifying lens longer lengthwise and a time comes when a creature underwater discovers that it craves air. It's being forced from familiar things for reasons it can only guess. It's made too much sense of its own patterns. Has found sigils and has cast them in the finding. Now it struggles with the last few breaths before whatever it breathes must be lighter. Its morphology craves ascending. Which, at times, is reaching for sunlight, at times, falling off into space. Depending upon which way the lens slides.

So it's larval. In time, its skin becomes dull for the sake of greater senses. The rippling world thickens to press in. Its instinct is to grow hard, to choke itself in its own fleshes until it can hack through the thickness and crawl into something light. Rip a glowing gateway into its own hardened skin and climb into the air something different. Where the hand of god waits to greet it and to guide it subtly about its way, humbling a procession of angels to bows. The greater order woven into its every cell is whispered on the first breeze that it breathes in a way that it's never breathed before.

It knows the wind first, of this new world, as the last of the water and fire debate. It cools as it dries and it associates the feeling with a sense of freedom. As it lightens as it grows. Following its urges and instincts with faith that it's intended. The sun, on its back, has a familiar warmth that the creature isn't ready to question. Its wings unfurl as they dry. Each wind gust makes them stiffen and stronger. Instructing with nudges that it's going to fly. More and more forcefully the closer they get to bearing their form. The closer they get to functional, the more the creature's body is forced to brace.

Its legs have dried too, in the light air, no longer needed to swim through thick water. They grow claws that grip against the tug of the wind. As its body hardens into its new form, new forces and shears tempt it with urges it doesn't yet understand. Strange new whims that threaten only elsewhere. It hesitates, holding a reed on a shoreline over calm waters rising. Feeling a pull it doesn't recognize enough yet to trust. Its inaction is not resistance, it's uncertainty. Old senses have quieted and new ones shout meaningless things. The world is white static as it stands atop the only thing and must decide in which direction to jump. Before it's torn free.

Its sense of self is different now. No matter what's left undone of its life's work after its life has drastically changed. A more clever creature could get all tangled up in the logic of that circumstance. Spend a thousand lifetimes, forgetting the one before, for the sake of perfecting its experience of the moment. A more clever creature would be able to conceive of perfection and would suffer in its absence. A damselfly need only be clever enough to sense the continuum. The path his life must follow so that he might dart quickly enough should the tide suddenly rise up around his legs.

The damselfly gasps and takes flight to this thought. Commits to the vector of onward before the breeze would've commanded it to. The ecstasy that follows is incidental. It coincides with the damselfly's first breath to make it a gasp or whatever it's equivalent. Suddenly air is its element anymore with the sun on its back. Its new sense of self craves congress.

J raises his hand and holds it in front of him. He waits as though he's been asked to. The sun's so high and bright that there are no shadows. The wind blows the damselfly up onto his finger. Its eyes are a million emeralds in a shimmering weave of gold above a mother of pearl bodice and iridescent glass wings. It's a map to all of the earth's treasures, as far as J can discern, down mineral hot springs, past crystal chambers, against tendrils of lava, reaching for the light. It's incredible what time has done.

Every passing moment is the culmination of a creature's life's work. J keeps this thought strong in his mind as he whispers what he won't write here, fearing each word would bind like an iron stitch on the page. He's uncertain because of what he's wished before. So he makes a wish that he must keep from being influenced by the wills of any others. He need only be heard by a damselfly. As he whispers to it, by the water, before he heads back to his way.

It flutters its wings, on his finger, and swats whatever words he says.

26. Everywhere is blue. J is blue. By now that should mean something. He understands that something has changed. His perspective has travelled fully into the future and everything he sees is backward. Like, but nothing like, his reflection. He's forgotten everything that failed to matter. It seems he remembers that the sky was blue. He assumes he's become the sky.

It's cloudy, on a sunny day, so there might be faces there to witness a man's last conversation with the world. They thunderstorm. J stands at the water's edge, where he's stood and left a thousand times, following echoes of siren's songs. He's tumbled down every mountain range to swim in every ocean. Each time, less unsure of what he'd done to get there, recognizing the place as an oracle would but never belonging there, until now. He's raced ahead to a place that waited for a better man's estimate of it.

This last day is different. There's no future beyond it. J has no sense of it Yesterday, he realized that he was further one way than any other and closer to the end than the beginning, he was sure. But there's no path that doesn't lead a man to his end no matter how lithe he is or how fine the balance. And J's the lucky one.

He's braced with ultraviolet tendrils in a blue world. And it's never clear which way through time he's travelling. It's okay to walk through the world feeling things. There's nothing more to a man than his sense of being. It's his creature's inclination to subdivide in order to make a whole. Not his own.

One sense - to feel. That is all. As to feel is to touch. As to feel is to be touched. Just on different levels. The feel of the sight of the sunlight. How it feels in the rain. A sense of sadness. Or of truth.

Says a lithe blue man who doesn't believe in entropy. Who fully refined his life, ridding himself of what isn't, and seeking out what is, important. Who wrote truths he did not intend and held his breath to endure the price of it. He became a conduit to hot things to exhaust his animal with the worst it could bear. Until now, now the worst is over and J's reward for bearing it is the power to calm.

A power he learned later than he might've used it. Instead, he held on as a wild thing bucked. Restrained it when he could not distract. Prayed he could hold on long enough by refusing to let go. Hold on long enough for the first chance to choke it, to tame his animal, by suffocation, when he's finally strong enough and brave enough to dare. Or if he's not, or if he must bear the bucking for other reasons, there are other ways to make a bucking thing surrender. Simply, a man only needs to find some other way to take away its breath. He must learn to command the wind and use it to summon wonders.

It took the full strength of J's libra. He dug a hole until he could dig no deeper. He jumped all the way in and climbed all the way out. Then climbed the mountain of dirt beside the hole and sits now by the sun. He's fully exhausted himself now and must find another source or finally attain one he's already found. Guided still by compulsion, only now, by the craving of his soul, he's built his vantage high enough to sense further than he has before.

He lets his tendrils drift off on the breeze to see what he'll glean from what they gather because to understand how the world's draped in light is to crave its vibration. Is to surrender to it. So he walks the lengths of what he senses and reaches for the sound like a tree would. He knows it's his job to stay behind to make sure that each man has made his choice before he might go about making his own.

It leads him to the water's edge where it reveals to him the path to the sun. Just before the night comes, he finds a way to say it so it's true. That he's the last man left after they've all disappeared. So there's no one left to stop him from walking across the water. He grunts to pull his rooted limbs free when he's finally able to withstand the pull, dragging him down, despite the lightness of his being. He has no roots yet, only feet, and begins to understand what he must feed on. He becomes the only earth and floats out to sea.

Chasing the sun with the full will of his crown. With the same white fire he used upon the world to turn everyone brilliant before he left. His yearning to be found beautiful again forced everyone else to see. So he could go off and chase the perfect orbit. Reduce every irrelevance to naught so he might learn enough to humbly worship two things in perfect balance.

Like the balance of the sea and the sun. Where there's room, at the flametips of a million degree fire, for a man's ribcage on a seafloor. Like the balance of the sea and the sky. Two planes to which he's the only point on every horizon. Like the balance of the sun and the night.

The harmony of all these things lets him forget to remember. He floats across the water until he simply stops. When he's reached the perfect spot directly below the sun. It's here that a greater instinct reacts. His power to calm, quells the ocean. It does this by stopping the spin of the earth. By making it the center of the universe as it was before all those cancerous wills got entangled and had no choice but to grow more complex. He's pulled it back to simpler times and keeps pulling.

Above the perfect glass, he reflects upon his life as he reflects upon the water. He stays in this place between two places for days. Which could be years because time doesn't matter. There's the single metronome of one sun rising. There's one heartbeat. There's only sky. This is the recombining of a cell dividing to understand the truth of halves. Of the nature of two making one. So he might sit alone with it for a moment. Recognize whatever he might to call to his other half or to anyone who's seen him. This only dreamed-of tangent to his life's purpose who'll walk beside him to its end.

Every time the sun sets, it does through deepening water. So that J's memory of it changes. It's a cue he takes from the reflection of the setting sun and his curiosity about what a sunset might seem like should the sun set under water. In water deep enough to hold it without revealing a plane that doesn't belong there. It feels like a step backward to see a thing divide. So he deepens the water not to see it.

Until, one day, when the sun doesn't set at all. He realizes that the whole world has turned to liquid. Suddenly, all that's left to know is vast and bottomless. He sees all of the earth sink and fall away. Plummet to a pinpoint till it's swallowed by its own shadow and disappears into a folded space.

What stirs within him feels like terror though it's really excitement that he's survived the night and is now full witness to the sun.

J lies flat, face down above the water, looking deep into its depth. Into what's sometimes a mirror, sometimes a lens at the sun. These years, all this time, it's been all he's worked to accomplish and now he sees the full truth when he looks at it. He feels its aspects completely.

Without a thought, he knows that some celestial shift has happened. Between him and the world and the sun. He would spend the time it takes to know their rhythms exactly, so he knows it without even asking. Time rewards only resolve. The mathematics of it are undeniable. He finds that the world now orbits him. He's not lying flat, face down above the water. He's standing in free space, facing the world at his side. Until it spins around his back, leaving him alone with what's before him. Audience of one.

He's become a zero-point ego center and his perspective, alone, defines what is and what's not. He's held the beginning and the end of all that's left of the universe. He now stands beside the water. Suddenly, he's the pivot of everything spinning, braced between sea and sky. Tracing the perfect circle of what used to spiral. From a viewpoint above, where there's only centrifugal balance. From a place where he can pull no more.

He's suddenly at the end of an infinity. The end of any cycling infinity is always perpendicular to its motivation. His reflection is his single fascination anymore. The depths of his shadow when the sun's overhead. The glare when it's eclipsed by glass.

Until the time comes, and the time always comes, when the sun shines no shadow at all. After he's told away the last of his person and has become transparent to the world. No longer distracted or distracting from what's going on since everyone can see right through him.

Though he's grown sedate to the rhythm and the singleness, he stirs quickly to note what's amiss. He looks into his reflection to find that he's been revealed as blue water, too. Just like the globe of the world. In the reflection of his reflection, he sees the infinity within what he's forsaken, like a ladder spiraling back down into it. Back ultimately to where he belongs.

The reflection of the sun has changed from what it was once. Or the way in which he senses it has changed. What was once only one man, and the two planes that reflect him, has become the juggling of three celestial spheres in an endless bluesky, vying for places in arrangements of continuums. Each shuffling from the beginning to the end to the one sphere forced to endure some moment on some path between the two. Now, fully aware of all the lures and entanglements when more than just a toe's dipped in.

There's fire and water and the will for this to be.

J dips in a toe. To feel what the sun feels like, at the instant the perfect alignment is achieved, and the sun's image pulses to fill the globe of the world. It feels all made of light. So, he closes his sense to anything other than the water. For as long as he does, there's only the complete satisfaction of watching ripples dilate then converge on the other side. While he sits on the border of several infinities, belonging to and subject to none. Anymore than any other spirit in the sky.

The ripples, as they circle the planet, extend like half-spheres deep down into it. Patterns fitted perfectly together, explained by a common source, like faces on a Russian doll nesting. It begins with balance, which becomes a rhythm, whose will compounds, and reaches for what might be reached for. J's just reversed it. Unwound the pattern as far as it would go. To witness the first drop of water think it might become a crystal flake of snow.

A man could grow complacent in that kind of serenity. If there was time. But there's no time here. So he's not surprised when a dolphin jumps clear from the liquid and flips overtop his head. He's felt the ripples of it coming, amongst other things, ever since the first of his tendrils suspected. Long before he dipped in a toe. It's the first of a fleet of them following, he senses. These are familiar creatures, surfing the fastest flows to where they'll run out of time. Before they fall back into it. Guided by the sense of a force much like gravity only older.

He recognizes them by the stuff they're made of. Beyond how they ripple to what beats within each growing ring. Beyond just patterns of patterns off by just a single dimension. Not really anything more than the flash of light they've seen in between. Where the truth opens just widely enough for each of them to see their reflection. Where they see and recognize new aspects to their expressions after the cloud's finally lifted and there's nothing left keeping the sea from the sky. So begins the urge to race, to jump for the sake of falling.

J waits for them. He's been barred from the sun by his choice so long as he chooses it. He's charged with the in-between and must choose to bear it. This momentary reprieve of duty is all he could do to get close enough to the source to believe. To bolster his belief, he needed to be left alone with it for a time. To understand that the fire and the water matter less than the force keeping them apart. The genesis. The will to be. He's spent his lifetime gathering courage beyond his conflicts. Collecting himself to pool in the center, a singularity. Made of water in the sun. Until he could go no further.

He now sits, the Libran sentry, beside the only thing and from where it came. He's been buried before, deep down below the water, under the seafloor, under the ocean. Then he clawed himself free of the skin of the earth and swam against riptides to breathe. Until implication led him further to a place where he was finally alone. Then left him alone there long enough to make the choice. The one his animal had to be trained to see with electric shocks and beatings.

He suffered all the right combinations of consequences, suspected and knew all the right things, to be filled overfull then emptied, in order to find room enough to become the perfect witcher beacon stepping-stone who could find his way to water, leave markers along the way and wait at the threshold to show others the sun.

To let them see that the moments of this life only matter so much, that this moment isn't important to those men who aren't living in it. It can be entered into and left without consequence. The same can be said for any circumstance of any day in the meantime. There's water and there's sun and a lifetime of enduring it. Those who are involved get easily captivated by all the things that the water and the sun can do. They can do such brilliant captivating things. Wonders. To an animal and his animus. Fueled by their sense of the space in between them, just on the tips of their tongues.

J's blood has pooled in the center for his entire life so far. He's swallowed every horizon to understand the extents of his experience so he might finally come to terms with it. It's time to feed his extremities and reverse his tentacles ability to feel. To use the sense of the things they've gathered to make of them a lifetime of days. There are sirens still in the water singing. This is the essence of life and how all life evolves. It senses something worth reaching for and becomes what it takes to grab.

So J reaches.

He remembers what it means to be a man. For all his time here, the night has gone and taken the last sleep with it. J's fought against the balance for long enough and must rest his soul's effort for the sake of his animal. The sunlight shines brightly everywhere, raising mountaintops on worlds of raindrips.

So back to it.

He hears a familiar song, across the water, sung by a man he's yet to know. It's his urge to follow concentric rings to join that man in chorus. To swim past racing dolphins to reach the core of what they've left behind. Where the voices of ghosts most clearly echo. Of the lives of men disappearing. To set feet again upon this perfect earth. To find and finally, together, wander free.

He plunges his face into the water and becomes one of us.